BARBARA SMITH

GREAT
Canadian
Ghost
Stories

LEGENDARY TALES OF HAUNTINGS

FROM COAST TO COAST

TOUCHWOOD

Edited by Claire Philipson
Designed by Colin Parks
Proofread by Warren Layberry

LIBRARY AND ARCHIVES CANADA CATALOGUING IN PUBLICATION

Smith, Barbara, 1947 April 19-, author

Great Canadian ghost stories : legendary tales of hauntings from coast to coast / Barbara Smith.

Issued in print and electronic formats.

ISBN 978-1-77151-279-4 (softcover).—ISBN 978-1-77151-280-0 (HTML)

1. Ghosts—Canada. 2. Haunted places—Canada. I. Title.

BF1472.C3S65 2018   133.10971   C2018-903455-6   C2018-903456-4

We acknowledge the financial support of the Government of Canada through the Canada Book Fund and the Province of British Columbia through the Book Publishing Tax Credit.

Canada Council for the Arts   Conseil des arts du Canada   BRITISH COLUMBIA   BRITISH COLUMBIA ARTS COUNCIL An agency of the Province of British Columbia

This book was produced using FSC®-certified acid-free paper, processed chlorine free, and printed with soya-based inks.

Printed in Canada at Houghton Boston

22 21 20 19 18   1 2 3 4 5

FSC
www.fsc.org
MIX
Paper from
responsible sources
FSC® C103214

With thanks to all the readers
who have accompanied me on my
"spirited" journey over the years

Contents

Introduction

As to ghosts or spirits, they appear totally banished from Canada. This is too matter-of-fact country for such supernaturals to visit.

—CATHARINE PARR TRAILL,
BACKWOODS OF CANADA, 1836

Canada's history and geography are haunted by classic ghost stories. This book is a collection of those supernatural tales. The stories are from every province and territory. Some of the tales are very old, while others include ghosts who are still active today—so active that people routinely say hello to them before getting on with their business.

The stories also reflect their own era and culture. For instance, no one knows first-hand what life during the Gold Rush was like, but, fortunately, through folklore, we can try to understand what life would have been like.

In choosing the stories for this book, I have tried to include accounts that reflect Canada's diverse cultures. Toward that end, you will find tales of haunted houses, a haunted theatre where a ghost is considered a member of the staff, phantom ships, haunted hotels, a possessed doll, and even the ghosts of murderers who are said to be seen hitchhiking into their afterlives. The one aspect that all of the stories have in common is that they have all been reported and recorded as actual events.

It has been my privilege over the years to write a series of books about true ghost stories. Not surprisingly, I am frequently asked, "What is a ghost?" I am sure that people asking that question expect I will have a ready answer for them. I sincerely wish I did. Some of the world's greatest minds have spent years pondering this subject without coming to any firm conclusions. As I do not regard myself as any sort of an expert but rather a collector of folklore, I feel no embarrassment at my lack of a stock answer.

In the context of the thousands of ghost stories I've been told, some theories explaining the existence of ghosts and haunted places do make more sense than others. For instance, Frederic Myers, one of the founding members of the old and honourable Society for Psychical Research in England, suggested in this book *Human Personality and Its Survival of Bodily Death* (1903) that a ghost is "an indication that some kind of force is being exercised after death," and that this force "is in some way connected with a person" now deceased.

Most other explanations are somewhat of a variation on this proposition. "Leftover energy" (physical or emotional) is a term used to describe the phenomenon that is a ghost. The "psychic imprint" theory holds that the essence of a person has been somehow stamped on the environment in which that person lived. The deceased person's soul has effectively left an imprint on the physical world.

Another theory holds that ghosts are disembodied souls (or energies or personalities or spirits) that are usually detectable only by our nearly atrophied sixth sense. Rather than perceiving this otherworldly sensation with our familiar five senses, we notice the hair on our arms or the back of our necks standing up on end, or a tingling sensation on our skin, or the feeling that we are being watched when we know we are alone.

Other students of the subject support the hypothesis that ghosts are deceased persons whose beings either do not know they are dead or cannot accept death because they feel obligated to complete unfinished business among the living.

Throughout all of these suppositions is the underlying question of whether a ghost originates with the living person who is experiencing the encounter or with the ghost itself. Perhaps that point is debatable, but because many people report seeing or sensing the same spirit either at the same time or at different times, that event is certainly more objective than merely a figment of "the mind's eye."

The most strikingly different aspect of all the theses is "retrocognition": seeing or sensing the past. Examples of retrocognition can be found in a story in this book entitled "Time Slips" (see page 195). Another concept of a ghost is almost the opposite: "forerunners" are ghosts that have predicted future events.

While some ghosts, such as forerunners, have messages for us, others just seem to be continuing about their business, oblivious to the world of the living that surrounds them.

Not all ghosts present themselves visually in the shape of humans. Although apparitions and poltergeists fall under the broad definition of the general term "hosts," they have some additional qualities. An apparition is a visible presence; it has a discernible physical form. While this form tends to be the popular conception of a ghost, a sighting of an apparition is actually a statistical rarity.

A poltergeist is an equally rare type of spectral being that can be identified by its noisy and possibly violent behaviours. It will often move objects and can actually wreak havoc on its surrounding physical environment. Poltergeists are strongly associated with people rather than places. They have been known to follow people for years, even through a succession of moves.

A ghost may be present only in the form of a sensation—a person feels that he or she is not alone although no one else is physically present. Ghosts can also manifest as smells, both pleasant and unpleasant. Other manifestations include ghostly lights and phantom music.

Some people are much more likely than others to encounter a ghost. It has been proposed that some of us are more attuned to the "wavelength" on which ghosts transmit. Although this sensitivity seems to be naturally occurring, it is also apparent that the ability can either be enhanced with practice or left to diminish.

Being haunted is not necessarily a permanent status for either a person or place. A place that is currently haunted may not always be so. Conversely, just because a home or workplace is a ghost-free zone today doesn't mean it always will be.

It seems that there are more questions than answers when it comes to ghost stories. Because these are true stories, they are not always neat and tidy with distinct beginnings and endings. They feel more ragged than a fictional account would, but for me, that is a part of the fun because I love both history and mystery. I hope you will enjoy reading this book as much as I have enjoyed writing it.

One final note: Please know that all my books of ghost stories, including this one, have been written to entertain and inform, not to change anyone's belief systems.

Happy hauntings!

NEWFOUNDLAND AND LABRADOR

Beloved Chief Called Away

The following legend is so old that most of the facts have been lost to the mists of time. The story that does remain tells us that people have seen a dramatic apparition on Glover Island in Grand Lake near Corner Brook, Newfoundland. The ghost is said to be that of a Beothuk chief who lived in the 1800s.

Not only did his own people hold him in great esteem, the leader also earned the respect of the Europeans who had come to settle and trade with the Indigenous People. On the day the chief made his last visit to the local trading post, he refused to take anything in exchange for the furs he had brought in with him. Instead, the man explained that he was elderly and that the Great Spirit had let him know that his days on earth were numbered. Then he turned and left the rough-hewn building.

A few days later, a trapper reported seeing the old man sitting in his canoe on the water near the shore of Glover Island. The leader's arms were crossed, his paddle was in his lap, and his colourful blanket was folded across his shoulders. He was gazing off into the distance. The trader called out a greeting, but the man in the canoe didn't respond. This was unlike the chief's usual warm behaviour, so the trader looked more closely, and that is when he knew something was very wrong. Impossibly, the chief's canoe was moving against the wind and waves.

It wasn't until the trader learned about the chief's last visit to the post that he realized he had likely witnessed the respected man's last few moments on earth. And, indeed, the old man was never seen alive again.

At first, everyone who knew the man mourned his death, but inevitably, over the years, people's memory of the great chief faded. That is when an inexplicable manifestation began to appear on the island. It was an image of an old man sitting calmly on a rock, a colourful blanket wrapped around his shoulders.

The manifestation seemed aware of his surroundings because he always turned his head toward approaching canoes. By the time the witnesses beached their canoes on the island's shore, the ghost was nowhere to be seen.

As the years went on, people noted that the apparition was becoming less and less clear until finally the ghost with the distinctive blanket faded from sight entirely.

Mysterious Rescue

We presume that all ghost stories are tales about the spirit or soul of someone who has died, but this is a ghost story with a difference—enough of a difference to make us question the reality we take for granted.

Icebergs off the eastern banks of Newfoundland have always been lethal threats to sailors and their ships. In the late autumn of 1823, the captain of a square-rigged barque guided his vessel through the final hours of a voyage from Liverpool, England. It had been a difficult passage. Provisions were low, and the crew was exhausted, but at last, the craggy shores of home were not far off.

About noon, the captain and his mate, Robert Brace, a young man from Torbay, Newfoundland, bundled up against the cruel cold and walked out onto the ship's deck. The freezing air all but took Brace's breath away, so the two were silent as they made their routine navigational observations and checks. Once they were back in the captain's quarters, the men conversed comfortably, comparing their assessments and working out the ship's position and progress.

The captain left Brace working and quietly went to attend to his duties elsewhere on the ship. But Brace hadn't heard his superior leave the room, and so he wasn't surprised when, out of the corner of his eye, he saw a man sitting at the captain's desk, hunched over his writing slate. No doubt the captain was still figuring out coordinates.

When he'd finished his own calculations, Brace turned to confirm his figures with the captain. Much to his shock, however, the man sitting at the desk was not the captain but a stranger, a person Robert had never seen before.

This can't be, Robert tried to assure himself. *We've been at sea for days. No one could have come aboard this ship, nor could anyone have remained hidden as a stowaway for this length of time.*

Brace called out to the man at the desk, demanding that he identify himself. The image remained silent, but he lifted his head from the slate he had been writing on and looked at Robert with eyes as cold as the North Atlantic seas that were buffeting the barque.

Brace's knees quaked, and sweat poured from his face. For a few moments, he was paralyzed with fear, but as soon as he was able to make his legs respond, he ran to find the captain.

"Who's in your cabin, writing at your desk?" the young man demanded when he found the officer.

"No one is there, as far as I know," the man replied, surprised. Robert Brace was one of his most trusted sailors and known to be a rational man. The captain didn't expect him, of all people, to be upset over some foolishness.

"There is a man sitting at your desk," Brace insisted.

"It must be one of the crew then, the second mate or possibly the steward. None of the others would go into my quarters without my permission."

"The man sitting at your desk and writing on your slate is no member of this crew. I have never seen this man before in my life, and yet he's aboard this ship," Brace exclaimed.

Not wanting to call one of his most trusted workers a liar, the ship's leader pointed out the obvious. "We've been at sea for nearly six weeks. Where could he have come from?" Then, realizing that his mate was well aware of those facts, the older man added, "Let's go below and find out."

The captain and Brace made their way back down to the quarters where the younger man had seen and spoken to the stranger. The room was empty. Nothing seemed to be out of place; nothing was missing. At first, it seemed as though no one had been in the room at all, then Robert noticed a message written in unfamiliar handwriting on the slate atop the captain's desk. The words "Sail for the northwest" had been neatly written across the surface.

"Did you write this?" the officer asked Brace.

"No, of course not," he replied. "You know what my handwriting looks like. It doesn't resemble this script at all. Did you write it?"

The captain apparently felt that last question did not even warrant and answer, for he simply turned and left the room. Nearly half an hour elapsed before he returned.

"I've checked the handwriting of everyone on the ship. None of them write this way. I make the assumption that we have a stowaway, and I've ordered a complete search of the ship," the older man informed Brace.

Although the crew searched the ship from port to starboard and bow to stern, no one was found. The captain was puzzled because he knew that Robert Brace was not the kind of sailor to make up a story about a stranger; besides which, the message on the slate seemed to confirm the young man's otherwise preposterous claim. There was no alternative but to investigate what this strange series of events could mean, and he ordered the ship's helmsman to steer to the northwest.

With all hands on deck, the ship veered in a new direction, the direction indicated by the mysterious message. Every man on board was acting as a lookout, they just weren't sure what they were looking out for. After an hour on the new route, no one had spotted anything unusual. It was the same after two hours, except that the seascape was more heavily dotted with icebergs, but other than those, the men saw nothing worthy of note.

They'd been sailing on their new course for more than three hours when they spotted what appeared to be the remains of a ship stuck fast in an ice field. When they approached as near as they dared, the sailors on the barque, Robert Brace included, could see that the trapped vessel was badly damaged. She was certainly not seaworthy and may actually have been abandoned.

Not knowing whether it was now a rescue mission or a salvage operation, the captain dispatched Brace and two other men in a lifeboat to approach the stranded ship. As they neared it, they could hear voices. People were obviously still aboard. When the trio in the lifeboat called out, their cries were answered by men scrambling around to the side of the deck nearest the approaching craft.

Waving madly, the men aboard the icebound vessel clearly indicated they needed help. "Thank God you're here," a figure from the deck shouted. "We couldn't have held out much longer. We're in imminent danger of sinking."

The rescue party steered the lifeboat over to a flat portion of an iceberg. The endangered sailors clambered down from their ship, crossed the ice, and boarded the rescuers' boat. As was fitting, the captain of the abandoned craft spoke first.

"We left Liverpool weeks ago, bound for Quebec. We'd been stuck between those ice floes for so long that we'd all but given up hope of being rescued. We owe you our lives. How did you happen to be navigating this exact course?" the rescued leader enquired.

"Bring your men below where it's warmer," the other captain replied. "We'll explain as best we can once we're in quarters."

Robert Brace greeted the men with a nod as they made their way below deck and out of the elements. Several of the rescued sailors had passed by when Brace saw him—the man who had been sitting in the captain's quarters writing on the slate. Brace stopped the sailor and asked, "Have you ever been aboard this vessel before?"

"No, of course not," the confused, cold, and badly shaken man replied.

"But I've seen you," said Brace. "I know I have. It was earlier today, just after noon. You were sitting at the captain's chair, writing on his slate. Then you disappeared, and we couldn't find you anywhere on board, but we did find your instructions to change our course. That's how we happened to spot your stranded ship," Brace explained.

"It could not have been me that you saw. Just after noon today, I was in my bunk trying to sleep. I don't think I ever lost consciousness completely. I did have a strange dream although I can't recall its nature. Until a few minutes ago, I'd been aboard the same ship since we left Liverpool," the stranger informed Brace.

"But even the other man's clothes were the same as yours," Brace muttered in astonishment before he went to find the captain. He'd have to explain the situation although he had no idea how he'd accomplish that without sounding like a fool.

The captain listened more patiently than Brace expected. Silently the older man took a spare slate down from a shelf and handed it to the stranger saying, "Humour me, please. Write something on this slate, write 'Sail for the northwest.'"

The man was clearly puzzled, but he did what he was asked and then handed the slate back to the rescue boat's captain who, in turn, compared it to the slate that had been on his desk. The handwriting was identical.

A stunned silence pervaded the room, and then the man who had written the lifesaving message on the slate—twice—spoke. "Now I think I remember some of my dream. I saw myself boarding another ship and pleading for help."

Somehow, the desperate man's mind had transported his spirit to the only possible chance for rescue. His spirit, his presence, his ghost, if you will, had travelled on a lifesaving mission to prevent his own death.

Amends in the Afterlife

No one knows exactly where or when Esau Dillingham was born. Despite this, it's a matter of historical record that by 1910 he was living a hard life in rugged rural Labrador and was known simply as "Smoker." That moniker wasn't chosen by chance. It was the generally accepted term for someone who made moonshine liquor, and that's exactly what Smoker did. He ran a still where he made alcohol—deadly alcohol—from spruce cones, sugar, and yeast. Not surprisingly, his quality control was questionable, but even so, he did a brisk trade that brought tragic results. Some of his customers went blind. Others went mad. Most became so dreadfully sick that they wished they were dead, and some actually did die from drinking his brew.

Lawmen were constantly on Smoker's trail, but he wasn't an easy man to catch because he had surrounded his illegal operation with bear traps—ones that didn't know the difference between a bear's leg and a constable's leg. Dillingham only left his encampment during the harsh Labrador winters, and when he did, he always wore a white fur coat and drove a team of pure white dogs, making himself all but invisible against the snow-covered background.

In 1920, Smoker's devious life caught up with him when he began to sample his own wares. Soon he went mad and murdered a man who had come to make a purchase. Too sick from his own brew, Smoker wasn't able to run. He was arrested and taken to a jail cell on Frenchman's Island. He died shortly thereafter. His dying words were to beg for forgiveness and the opportunity to atone for his evil ways.

Not long afterward, a trapper trading from a nearby post had an amazing story to tell. He'd been travelling with his dog team through a raging blizzard when he realized he was hopelessly lost. Just then, the image of a man dressed in white furs with a team of pure white dogs suddenly appeared at his side. The mysterious driver and his team guided the trapper to lifesaving shelter before disappearing into the whiteout. After that initial sighting, Smoker's ghost was seen often.

In 1949, two RCMP officers, George Bateson and Ed Riopel, were stationed at the Labrador outpost of Frenchman's Island. One winter's day as they made their way on dogsled back to their quarters, they encountered a fierce blizzard. The wind blew razor-sharp ice particles against the few centimetres of flesh exposed around the men's eyes. Snow blindness seemed inevitable and death by freezing probable.

They had all but given up hope when they caught sight of a white dog team and a driver clad in white furs. They called out to him, but he didn't respond. In desperation they altered their course to follow the silent, indistinct vision. Their dogs were exhausted but somehow managed to keep going. Then, just for a moment, the wind died down enough for the constables to see a small cabin not far in the distance. There was smoke billowing from the chimney. Their lives were saved. As they steered the dogs toward the shelter, the wind picked up again, and their white-clad escort vanished.

Trappers who had set up camp in the cabin to wait out the storm welcomed the nearly frozen men. Once the officers had eaten and slept, they explained how they had come to find the cabin.

One of the Mounties added that they must make an effort to find the Good Samaritan who had guided them to safety and let him know what a good deed he had done.

A trapper who was piling more logs on the fire turned to the survivors and told them, "You'll never find that one on this side of the veil. That was Smoker, and he's been dead for more than thirty years."

The officers sat in stunned silence. The ghost of a repentant murderer had saved them. Esau Dillingham's life was full of evil, but he had kept to his dying proclamation and devoted his afterlife to righteousness.

The Isle of Demons

In 1515, Marguerite de la Rocque was born into France's high society. As she was growing up, she must have received all the pampering that money and privilege could provide, but the protected life was not for Marguerite. When she was in her mid-twenties, she left her comfortable home in Europe to accompany her uncle Jean-François on a voyage to the New World.

During the long and dangerous days at sea, Marguerite had only her servant, Damienne, for company—until she fell hopelessly in love with a young man on board, Etienne Gosselin. By all accounts, Etienne was a handsome lad who often entertained those aboard with his music. How could a young lady resist? Unfortunately, Marguerite's uncle saw no charm in the budding relationship, and he forbade the two from seeing each other. But his threats weren't equal to the energy of young love, especially in such cramped quarters. Jean-François was furious when he discovered that his niece had disobeyed him, but he did nothing until the ship had sailed to an island north of today's Newfoundland.

This was no ordinary island. The small rocky outcropping was known as the Isle of Demons, and no sailors, no matter how brave they were, would ever go ashore because this place was as close as one could get to the gates of Hell. The island was deserted, except for wild beasts, demons, and the tortured souls of sailors who had died at sea.

And that is exactly where Jean-François left his niece, along with her servant, Damienne, and of course, Etienne Gosselin, with only a few meagre supplies and a couple of rifles.

Stranded in this terror-filled place, the three struggled to stay alive by hunting bears or any other wild animals they could. They ate what they could of the beasts and used the pelts to protect themselves from the frigid North Atlantic winds. At night they would try not to hear the wails and howls of the long-dead sailors.

Soon Marguerite realized she was pregnant. By the time the baby was born, both Etienne and Damienne had died. Marguerite knew that she had to get away from this cursed island. Whenever she saw a ship off in the distance, she would run to the shore and signal as energetically as she could. Sometimes a ship would stop, but even those vessels kept their distance because the sailors presumed that the madly gesticulating woman was one of the many evil apparitions haunting the Isle of Demons.

Marguerite's son only lived for a few weeks. The grieving mother knew she had to make a choice. She could either give up and follow her loved ones to an early grave, or she could redouble her efforts to save herself. She chose the latter and once again began signalling to every ship she saw. Finally, a fishing boat stopped close enough to shore that she could call out to it. The fishermen weren't convinced that she was a human being, but even so they were brave enough to sail closer and then send a landing party ashore. More than two years had passed since Marguerite had been cast away. No one would have recognized her as the fine young woman of privileged upbringing who had left France in 1542. The fishermen took her back to her family, where she recovered from her hideous experiences and presumably never ventured out on the Atlantic Ocean again.

Over the years, Marguerite de la Rocque's story has inspired plays, poems, nonfiction books, and even novels.

Today you won't find the Isle of Demons marked on any maps, but among the group of islands known as Îles Harrington, there still is a small island just off Newfoundland's north coast that no one will set foot on for fear of disturbing the many souls who haunt the rocky outcrop.

Ghostly Prediction

Summer is always a good time for a trip to visit the folks. And that is exactly what Bjarni Herjólfsson was doing in the year 985 when a vicious storm blew his longboat off course on route from Norway to Iceland. Once the weather cleared, Herjólfsson and his oarsmen were relieved to see land, but the land they saw was heavily forested and definitely not Iceland. The leader ordered his crew to change the ship's course immediately in hopes that they could make it to their intended destination before their supplies ran out.

It was a tense voyage, but they did arrive. As soon as Herjólfsson was safely inside his parents' home, he told them the story of the storm and about seeing the strange land that no other Norseman had ever seen. Herjólfsson's descriptions of the adventure spread quickly. Over the years, the tale was told so often that the details became entrenched in Viking folklore, and it was considered nothing more than a myth, another of the Norse sagas. Today, however, experts believe that Herjólfsson was the first European to see the eastern shores of Canada.

Seafaring was in the Vikings' blood, and tales like Herjólfsson's must have been enticing to those who came after him. So enticing, in fact, that three generations of explorers, first Thorwald Ericsson, then his son Eric the Red, and then his grandson Leif Ericsson all made journeys to the New World. They even established a colony on Newfoundland's shore and called it Vinland.

The settlement wasn't peaceful. There were constant battles between the Vikings and the people who had called that land home for many generations. During one of those clashes, Thorwald was killed. Leif and the others buried the man near their encampment. When Thorstein, the Ericsson brother who had stayed with his wife in Iceland, heard of Thorwald's death, he, his wife, and two dozen oarsmen set out for Vinland, determined to bring the body home. He didn't succeed, but he died trying.

Even so, the story of Thorstein and his wife was far from over. Just after his heart stopped beating, the man suddenly sat up and asked for his wife. She hurried to his side just in time to hear him predict that she would remarry and enjoy a long life as a Christian woman. The widow did exactly that, so whether the deceased man had seen her future or suggested it to her could be debated. It is also possible that the strange incident was added to the story later, when the Christian faith spread through the Norse culture. If not, then this may be the first recorded instance of communication from the afterlife associated with Newfoundland, but certainly not the last.

Visitors from the Past

The oldest recorded sighting of a phantom ship near Canada is that of a Norse longship. Way back in the 1920s, people standing near the shore of Placentia Bay, Newfoundland, looked out across the water and saw a vessel resembling an ancient Viking warship. This was especially puzzling because, at that time, no one knew that Norse explorers had ever travelled to North America. What was even more disconcerting was that the boat was engulfed in flames and the men aboard were screaming in pain and fear. The fire was so intense that the witnesses reported feeling its heat. Before any of those folks could decide what to do or how they could help, the image of the burning boat vanished without a trace. That fiery ship has never been reported since. Hopefully those pitiful souls have found their eternal rest away from tormenting flames.

Several other ghost ships, however, have been seen.

After a long day of fishing, a Newfoundland fisherman stood in a small hut sorting his catch when he heard an odd splashing sound coming from the water nearby. He was anxious to finish his work and get home to a hot meal, so he disregarded the noise and continued with the job at hand. A few minutes later, though, an ear-splitting blast, like a trumpet call, did get his attention. He looked out the shelter's door, but at first all he could see was a blanket of fog. Then he squinted his eyes and made out a small movement within the mist. Thinking that a fellow fisherman might be in danger, he walked to the shore where the waves crashed against the rocks. Whatever he had seen moving in that fog bank was getting closer. Moments later, a vision of a Viking warship emerged from the eerie darkness. The image was so clear that the man could make out the rows of oarsmen at each side of the boat. Paralyzed with fear, he watched the apparition until it faded from sight as mysteriously as it had appeared.

Although terrifying, that incident paled in comparison to another reported sighting some years later. A crew of fishermen was out on the water fishing when dark clouds started bruising the sky. Then a gale-force wind blew up. The men knew they had to get back to shore, quickly. Fighting back panic, the captain tried to start the boat's engine, but no matter what he tried, the motor refused to turn over. He and his men were in serious trouble. This storm was clearly a vicious one, and it was moving their way.

Before the captain could think of what to do next, he heard the distinctive sound of oars cutting through the whitecaps. Such relief. Someone was coming to rescue them. The fishermen strained their eyes toward the splashing. What they saw did nothing to calm their nerves, for there was an ancient Norse vessel heading directly for them.

What to do? The only way out would be to jump into the roiling ocean, and that would have meant certain death. But what other option was there? If that strange ship rammed theirs, they would be tossed into the frigid water anyway. The longship was nearly upon them. The captain only had a split second to make up his mind. Then, with a blast from the Vikings' war horn, the image of the ship broke up and disappeared into the fog.

Then the fishermen knew they were dealing with an element more unpredictable and more dangerous than weather. They were dealing with the supernatural. The captain tried his boat's engine again. This time it started! He and the crew made it back to shore, but they were badly shaken. Once they calmed down, they told their friends on the dock what they had just been through. The listeners nodded in sympathy. They had all heard tales of the Norse ghost ships.

Only two men, though, knew first-hand what the others had been through, and they chose that moment to confess to a crime they had tried to commit many years before. Knowing that a particular man kept liquor in his fishing hut, they broke into the cache and were about to make off with their spoils when they heard a disturbance out on the water. They looked out to see an enormous Viking ship sailing straight to shore. They dropped the bottles they'd intended to steal and ran for the town. Neither man had ever spoken of their encounter until that day.

Phantom ship sightings haven't been the only ghostly traces along the coastlines of Newfoundland and Labrador. People have reported hearing battle horns and war cries from inland. It's presumed that these are aural imprints from the numerous battles the Vikings had against the people whose land they were invading.

Another sighting took place in 1981, near the end of June. A group of tourists visiting the area of L'Anse aux Meadows, near the Vikings' former colony, gave detailed reports of seeing a ghost ship heading their way. This might have been put down to people being eager to share an unusual experience except there was an extraordinary twist: just three weeks earlier, other tourists, these ones visiting the shores of Iceland, had also seen a detailed apparition of a Norse ship. The phantom was so clear that they were able to make out the wretched crew and bearded captain, all dressed in animal hides. This ship was just heading out on its three-week voyage to the New World. The descriptions of the ship were virtually identical so, given the time lapse, it's been speculated that the Viking boat seen leaving Iceland was the same one seen arriving in North America roughly three weeks later.

Perhaps those with seafaring in their souls never give up the adventure.

Signal Hill

Cabot Tower on Signal Hill stands guard over St. John's, the capital city of Newfoundland and Labrador. It is said that the ghost of a broken-hearted young woman whose child died one bitterly cold night haunts the hill. That grieving mother is not alone in her afterlife. The spirits of women whose husbands never came back from sea are also thought to line the edge of the hill.

A Train to the Afterlife

Buchans and Millertown are two small communities nestled in Newfoundland's interior. From 1927 until the late 1980s, a railway 35 kilometres long linked the two towns. This was no passenger line. This was a railway built solely to transport zinc, lead, and copper from the mines in Buchans to Millertown. Although some sections of train track may remain, not one train has travelled that route since 1989—unless you count the phantom trains.

People near the track beds have seen a light in the distance. As they watch, the light becomes larger and brighter. This must be a train's headlight, they might surmise, except they know trains have not run in central Newfoundland for decades. They are seeing a phantom train, a supernatural memory of what once was.

Swamp Hag

Bell Island lies off the coast of Newfoundland in Conception Bay and has been called Canada's X-Files Isle. One of the strangest stories from the island dates back to World War 11, when a young woman was out walking along the coastline. She happened to see German U-boats being restocked close to shore. One of the German sailors noticed the girl and captured her. Certain that she would reveal their secret location, the submariners dragged her to a nearby marsh. Just before dying and sinking beneath the mire, the girl screamed for help. But if any people heard those cries, they were afraid to respond. The swampy marsh was thought to be home to evil spirits who cried out to attract any unwary person who happened by.

It is said that, even today, people can hear her mournful cries for help, but few have been unlucky enough to actually see her apparition, now known as the Swamp Hag. One man who did have that misfortune was Nathaniel Hammond. He had been working alone in a communal garden plot when a dreadful stench assaulted his nostrils. He looked around, but he couldn't see anything that might have caused the terrible, overpowering smell. As Hammond started to run for home, he found he was completely paralyzed by the stench. He dropped to the ground, nearly unconscious.

Soon a horrible female form crawled toward him. Her clothes were in tatters, her skin was peeling away, and her eyes were empty sockets, but the worst of this ugly apparition was her putrid smell. It was as if she had lain in a swamp for years and years. He tried to pick himself up and run away, but it was hopeless. He had no strength left. The ugly entity hissed in his ear, accusing the community of ignoring her dying pleas for help because of a foolish belief in superstitions.

Back at home, Hammond's wife was worried. She couldn't imagine what had kept her husband out this late. The woman ran to get Nathaniel's brother, and together they began to search for the missing man. When they finally found him, they could not even go near him. He smelled as though he had swamp water running through his veins.

Nathaniel Hammond eventually recovered, but it is no wonder that children on Bell Isle are warned not to go near the swamp for fear the hag's angry stench will steal them from their families.

NOVA SCOTIA

A Brother's Visit

On the evening of October 15, 1785, two young army officers, Captain John Sherbrooke and Lieutenant George Wynyard, settled into their barracks at Sydney on Cape Breton Island, Nova Scotia. They warmed themselves by the fire in the main room, each reading quietly by lamplight. When John felt a shiver run through his body, he told his friend that he'd be heading for the warmth of his bed soon. George didn't reply, and John wondered if his friend had fallen asleep in his chair.

But George was awake and sitting bolt upright in his chair. "His face was as pale as death," John noticed before he turned his head to look where George was staring.

John could hardly believe his eyes. A man was standing in front of them, but surely that couldn't be. They'd have known if someone else had come into the cabin. The presence stared at George; then it vanished. The two men were speechless. When George could find his voice he told his partner, "That was my brother."

"How can that be?" John questioned. "Your brother's at home in England."

George nodded. Indeed, as far as he knew, his brother was back in England. But if that were so, then how could he suddenly have appeared across the Atlantic Ocean in Nova Scotia? Of course they knew he couldn't have, so the captain and the lieutenant hurried outside to chase down the prankster who'd somehow disguised himself so cleverly and slipped into their cabin.

Unfortunately for the men's peace of mind, they found nothing indicating that the door to their room had been opened. The two agreed to keep their eerie experience to themselves, but George noted it in his journal. That didn't ease the man's mind though, and he became determined to solve the puzzle of the mysterious vision he and John had seen.

George sent a letter home to England, asking if there was any family news, but months went by with no response. When news finally did come it was in a letter to John, asking him to please tell George that there had been a tragedy. George's beloved younger brother had died the previous October. Quickly calculating the time difference between Canada and England, John realized that the spectre that he and George had seen had appeared at the very moment of the young man's death.

George Wynyard mourned for his brother, but he still managed to make such a success of his life that some said it was as though he was trying to live two lives. He served as a colonial governor and was knighted in recognition of his services. Throughout his long and productive life, the memory of seeing his brother's apparition that October night in 1785 never left him. George was an old man when he died. Hopefully the spirit of his brother was waiting for him.

Esther's Story

Life was simple for the people of Amherst, Nova Scotia, during the late 1800s. At least it was until September 1878, when word began to spread through the village that one of their own, eighteen-year-old Esther Cox, was enduring a series of utterly terrifying events. Some townsfolk even whispered that an unnatural force had possessed the girl.

When the local minister, a man named Temple, heard about Esther's trouble, he decided to pay her a call. The young woman lived with her sister Olive and Olive's husband, Daniel Teed, two of her siblings, Daniel's brother, and Daniel's two small sons. The house might have been crowded, but they were all good, upstanding citizens, well liked and respected in the community.

As the Reverend Temple made his way toward the family's small home, he was only mildly apprehensive. His experience with such domestic upheavals told him that if there were a problem in the home, it would be of a practical nature. Initially, the minister's confidence increased when Daniel greeted him at the door and ushered him into the kitchen, the room traditionally used for somewhat informal visiting.

But, once he was inside, Temple could see that Daniel did not look well. The man's face was pale and drawn. Circles darkened the skin under Daniel's eyes, and he had lost a noticeable amount of weight in only a few days. The state of the house was even more concerning than Daniel's appearance. Olive Teed usually kept the place neat and orderly, but now it was chaotic. Kitchen utensils and pieces of paper were littered about. A bucket of water from the outside well stood on the kitchen table. Not only was this unlike the Teeds' regular habits, it was against the community's accepted standards of sanitation. The minister hoped that his reaction to the all these incongruities wasn't apparent. He was there, after all, to bring the family comfort, not to judge their habits. Esther, the focus of the man's visit, was nowhere to be seen.

Daniel waved his hand toward an empty chair at the table, and the minister lowered himself onto the hard seat. The two men were barely settled when a strange noise, a bubbling, came from the offensive water bucket. Temple swung his gaze toward the sound. At first, he couldn't believe his eyes. It actually looked as though the water inside the rough-hewn container was moving. *That's impossible*, he thought, as he stared at the liquid. Seconds later, the water began to boil furiously. Reverend Temple fled from the house in terror and never returned. But whatever unnatural force was causing the water to spontaneously boil tortured various members of the family for nearly two years.

The trouble had begun after Esther Cox went on a date with a man named Bob McNeal who worked with Daniel at the local shoe factory. To say that Esther and Bob's date did not go well would be an enormous understatement. The outing began with Bob driving Esther to a secluded spot outside the town limits in his horse-drawn buggy. Once they were away from prying eyes, he tried to have his way with the girl. When she refused to cooperate, he threatened Esther at gunpoint. Fearing for her life, Esther ran away as quickly as she could.

Once she was safely home, the traumatized young woman headed straight for bed, too humiliated to tell anyone what had happened. All she could hope was that by morning, the intensity of the awful memory would have diminished and she would be better able to cope. For now, all she wanted was to pass into the only oblivion available to her: sleep. She crawled onto the straw-filled mattress that she shared with her sister Jane and pulled up the covers.

Sadly, Esther's attempt to escape her problems failed. She slept fitfully as dreadful images tormented her mind. She felt as though something was crawling up her arms and legs, and there were mysterious scraping noises under the bed.

The next night was no better. Esther's mind was full of haunting images. She feared that something was in the bed, but it wasn't until Jane screamed in terror that Esther knew for certain these feelings were not merely figments of her imagination. Jane had also felt and seen a snake-like movement under the covers, and the sounds from under the bed persisted.

The two girls huddled together in fear for a moment, and Jane suggested that a mouse might have worked its way into the box of quilting squares stored beneath their bed. Together, they pulled the box of material out into the open. As they knelt to rummage through the pieces of cloth, the carton rose from the floor and rotated, top to bottom, in mid-air. The cotton contents fluttered prettily to the floor in a silent, brightly coloured display of ghostly power.

Jane's shrieks woke the family, and Daniel came running. He laughed at the sight that met his eyes and told the girls to tidy up the mess, get back to bed, and not disturb him again because, in case the two silly young women were not aware, Daniel needed his sleep. He had to work the next day, and the shop was short-staffed. Bob McNeal had not been at work for two days, and no one had been able to find him.

The third night that Daniel was woken by screams, however, he did not dismiss what he found in the girls' bedroom. Jane stood beside the bed, one arm covering her eyes, the other extended toward Esther. Esther was nearly unrecognizable. Her body had levitated from the bed. She was swollen and hideously disfigured and her exposed skin had turned a horrid, unnatural shade of red. Daniel screamed for his wife to join him. As Olive entered her sisters' bedroom, Esther's body suddenly deflated and fell back onto the bed.

Later, none of them could speak of what they had seen. Not only did they not want to frighten the others, they were also afraid that such talk would somehow make their fears more real. Each of the four, Esther included, suspected that the girl had become possessed.

Their suspicions were confirmed by the end of the week. Sheets, quilts, and blankets rose from Esther and Jane's bed and stayed stationary for only a moment before throwing themselves across the bedroom and landing on the floor in the corner.

Out of desperation and fear, the family called in the town's most respected citizen. Thomas Caritte, the local doctor, diagnosed Esther as having a severe case of "nerves." The word was no sooner out of the man's mouth than the girl's pillow and blankets flew off the bed again. As the doctor and the others stared in horrified helplessness, the words "Esther Cox, you are mine to kill" appeared on the bedroom wall.

Before hurrying from the room, Dr. Caritte administered a strong sedative to Esther. The tormented young woman fell into a deep sleep under the mysterious threat against her life.

Esther was the only one in the household who was able to sleep. The others were kept awake not only by fear but also by strange noises coming from the vegetable cellar. Daniel crept down the steps to see what was making the commotion. He retreated quickly when he saw potatoes flying around the dark space and heard loud knocks echoing from the roof of the house. This was all more than Daniel could take. He was too exhausted and fearful to go to work, which meant the family lost his much-needed wages. To make matters worse, his employer at the factory was not sympathetic because now he was short by *two* workers. Bob McNeal had still not shown up for work, and no one in town had seen him for several days.

When the sedative the doctor had given Esther finally wore off, she confessed that Bob had tried to attack her, and that he had even held a pistol to her head.

"Bob McNeal's spirit must be causing all of this," Jane Cox concluded. The words were no sooner out of her mouth than the family heard three distinct knocks on the bedroom wall. It was as if the forceful being was responding to Jane. Was the entity watching them and listening to everything that was going on in the house? If so, perhaps they could communicate with the spirit and drive it away.

Painstakingly, the desperate family worked out a system, a code of knocks, one bang meant "no," two meant "possibly," and three, "yes."

But the presence refused to leave.

Days of horror turned into weeks of horror, and Daniel decided that, for the sake of the rest of the family, Esther would have to be sent somewhere else to live. But just when those arrangements were being finalized, the young woman contracted diphtheria. For weeks she lay in enforced isolation, suffering with the highly infectious disease. Oddly, while she was sick, the supernatural acts stopped completely. Could they dare to hope that the terror was over?

As Esther began to recover from her illness, the sight of her familiar surroundings brought back horrible memories of how she had suffered with the cruelty of whatever supernatural force had haunted her. It was agreed that she should recuperate in Sackville, Nova Scotia, where another of her married sisters lived. While she lived there, Esther's life was quiet. Even at the Teeds' little house, the supernatural activity had finally given way to peace.

Feeling that life could finally get back to normal, Esther returned home to Amherst, but so did the spirit—with a vengeance. It made flames dance about her bedroom, lighting her clothes on fire.

"Are you trying to burn the house down?" Jane shouted at the invisible arsonist. "Knock, knock, knock," came the affirmative reply. Fearing for their lives, the family sent Esther away again. This time a local restaurant owner took the banished girl. He paid a high price for his kindness. After his business was damaged by increasingly strong poltergeist activity, he too sent Esther away.

A group of people from Saint John, New Brunswick, offered to take Esther in. They were not concerned about the poor woman's well-being but curious about the paranormal activities that seemed to follow her. As if out of spite for these ulterior motives, the presence became dormant. This respite from her tormentor, combined with her hosts' interest in the subject matter, gave Esther a chance to assess and even discuss her recent horrible experiences.

She explained to her hosts that she was sure spirits had taken up residence in her body. One, she said, was the soul of Maggie Fisher, a former schoolmate who had died. The other two entities were male. Esther didn't know one of them, but she called the other Bob Nickle, which was thought to be the poorly disguised revenant of her attacker, Bob McNeal. Unfortunately for Esther's peace of mind, the people who had taken her into their home for such selfish reasons soon became bored with her. They too sent her away.

Meanwhile, the Teed house was quiet. Daniel desperately wanted to keep it that way, so he found a family willing to employ his sister-in-law as a domestic aide. The arrangement worked well, except that Jane and Olive missed having Esther living with them. They convinced Daniel to let her come back home. She did, but not to stay. No sooner was Esther back in the house than the thumps on the walls and roof began again. She hadn't even had a chance to unpack her belongings.

The next family to take her in threw the anguished girl out when their barn mysteriously caught fire and burned to the ground.

Esther's plight and the bizarre state of affairs in Amherst had, by then, made headlines around the world. Among those whose attention it attracted was an American magician named Walter Hubbell. He proposed that he stay in the already crowded and tumultuous Teed home in order to exorcise the spirit that had possessed poor Esther's body and, by extension, her life and the life of her family.

Rain pelted down the afternoon Hubbell arrived in Amherst. The hopeful magician had barely set a foot toward the Teeds' front door when something ripped his umbrella from his hands. Once he was inside, a kitchen knife flew through the air directly at him. He ducked down just in time and the weapon missed its target. This seemed to anger the spirit even more, and furniture in the house began to move around. The knocks that the family had used to communicate with the spirit began pounding madly. Apports (small objects of unknown origin) began appearing in the home, and other objects, mundane ones such as a sugar bowl, disappeared.

By then even Hubbell knew he was into something well beyond his understanding. What he did understand, however, was how and why to draw a crowd. The showman was sure that the phantom's hijinks would draw paying customers and make him a tidy profit. He proposed turning Esther, and whatever possessed her, into something of an amusement park sideshow. Reluctantly, Esther and her family agreed to the man's plan. The spirit, however, clearly wanted no part of this commercial exploitation. In show after show and town after town, Esther Cox sat on an empty stage, dressed in a bizarre costume, amid complete peace and tranquility. The spirit was mute and motionless. Hubbell resorted to trickery, making objects fly around the girl as she sat on stage, but it was clear to even the most naïve witnesses that Hubbell had merely perpetrated a hoax. Eventually, customers stopped showing up, and the man-made plans to move on to other, hopefully more lucrative, endeavours.

Before he left, whether out of kindness or because he didn't want anyone else to be able to profit from Esther's situation, he took her to a community of neighbouring Micmacs. A medicine man from Pictou, Nova Scotia, succeeded where European medicine, magic, and Christianity had failed. Esther Cox was finally cleansed of the manifestation that had inhabited her.

Hubbell, not content to let his experiences be completely profitless, published a book variously known as *The Great Amherst Mystery* or *The Haunted House*. People were fascinated, and the book sold well for years, which brought Hubbell the profit he had sought.

Once she was free of Hubbell, Esther found a job working on a farm, but her employment only lasted until the phantom's flames burned the barn to the ground. She was convicted of arson and served a month in jail. It wasn't until December of 1879, fifteen months after her haunting began, that she was finally free of the spirit.

Shortly after that, Esther Cox married, had two sons, and then died in her early fifties. The source of the horrors she and her family suffered for nearly two years has never been determined.

Bob McNeal was never seen or heard from again. Some people wonder if the incident that initiated Amherst's supernatural mystery, Esther's unhappy date with McNeal in September of 1878, might have ended in his suicide or even murder. If Esther had been able to wrestle McNeal's pistol around, she could have shot and killed him. Perhaps after Esther fled, McNeal realized the implications of what he had done and killed himself. Or he might simply have left town, fearful that Daniel Teed would come after him, angry that he had made unwanted advances to Esther.

No matter what the reason might have been, Bob McNeal never reappeared at the shoe factory or anywhere else. No one can ever know for certain, but it does seem likely that McNeal's rebuffed advances toward Esther and the intense paranormal activity were connected.

This old but exceedingly well-documented ghost story is a classic example of a poltergeist infestation, and it has become a staple of Canadian folklore.

Mahone Bay

Oak Island is one of dozens of islands in Nova Scotia's Mahone Bay. Its initial distinction lay in the fact that it was the only island in the bay not covered in spruce and pine trees. Since then, however, Oak Island has also distinguished itself as being home to one of Canada's most enduring mysteries: Is there untold wealth buried somewhere on this small island?

There are dozens of excellent books and even a long-running television series dealing with the Oak Island treasure hunt, so the focus here will be on the island's ghost stories, some of which go back to a time well before the first treasure hunter set foot on the island in 1795.

European settlement around Mahone Bay began in the mid-1700s when immigrants from the United Kingdom and France left their homes and boarded woefully inadequate ships to sail across the Atlantic Ocean into the unknown. Those who made it arrived to harsh conditions and political unrest. Clearly, these were hardy people, and yet right from the start they were terrified of Oak Island, that small outcropping of land that lay so close to their shore. They knew the island was uninhabited, but they also knew that some nights they saw lights flickering in the forest of oak trees. Occasionally the settlers could even hear men's voices calling to one another. Eerier still, the brightness of those mysterious lights sometimes illuminated another extraordinary sight: men dressed in ragged clothes from a long-ago era. Oak Island soon took on a reputation of being an unnatural place, and tales of evil spirits haunting the island became commonplace.

One particular night, the villagers huddled in their rough-hewn houses as rain and hail pelted down. When they looked out across the water, they saw dark shapes moving among the oak trees and lights flickering eerily about the island. The next morning, two young fishermen from the town decided that something had to be done, and they set out in a small rowboat, determined to thoroughly explore Oak Island. Those brave, or foolish, men were never seen again. Nor was any trace of their boat ever found.

The people of the village mourned the loss and supported the missing men's families as best they could, but no one wanted to dwell on the tragedy because it was always there, just across the bay from them: the sinister, restless reality of that life-stealing island.

The terrible lure of the Oak Island treasure hunt began in the late eighteenth century. Daniel McGinnis, a young settler in the area, ignored his community's folklore and visited the island. As he walked through the forest, he noticed a circular depression of land in a clearing with a scarred tree at its edge. It was obvious that the tree's scars had not occurred naturally. It looked as though they could have been caused by a branch of the oak tree being used as a fulcrum for a pulley.

The sight was enticing. Daniel, like all the settlers in that area, knew the stories about pirates from long ago burying their treasure on the many islands scattered about the local bays. Thinking that he may have stumbled upon one of those caches, Daniel enlisted the help of two friends. The next day, full of enthusiasm and hope, the lads began digging, beginning a futile task that is still carried on by others to this day.

That trio, and those who came after them, uncovered a pit consisting of sharply perpendicular walls and a descending series of oak platforms. The existence of the pit certainly explains the depression Daniel found in the clearing, and the platforms laid every 3 metres down explain the clearing itself, as the oak trees must have been chopped down to build those platforms.

It was evident that a great deal of precise, painstaking, and gruelling work had been done, and that whoever had dug the pit had something valuable to hide. By the early 1800s, treasure hunters had made their way nearly 30 metres straight down. Fittingly, the excavation came to be known as the Money Pit.

The prospectors' progress was abruptly stopped when they dug down to a rock blocking the pit. It was a rock unlike any other they'd ever seen in the area. More puzzling still, this rock was inscribed with unfamiliar hieroglyphics. The entire mystery might have been solved that day, but night had fallen, so they postponed any further work until the next morning. By then it was too late. The pit had flooded. The treasure seekers began bailing out the shaft as best they could, but it was hopeless. Water was pouring in faster than they could bail it out, so they left that excavation and began the backbreaking work of digging another shaft nearby. That one flooded too, and by then they had run out of money.

Sometime during this fruitless activity, a gruesome myth was born that proclaimed the treasure would not be found until the oak trees were all gone and seven men had died. By then most of the trees were gone, and six men had been killed attempting to uncover the cache. Despite the imminent threat of that curse, the next generations of treasure hunters picked up where the defeated had left off; on it went through the centuries.

For efficiency, prospectors and their families began living on Oak Island. Peggy Adams was the three-year-old daughter of one of the families that had moved to the island in 1940. The Adams family home was a shack, virtually isolated from the outside world. One winter's day, the little girl came running back shortly after her mother sent her out to play. Peggy told her mother she had seen strange men on the beach. "They were wearing pretty clothes. The men's trousers had stripes down the sides, and their jackets were red."

Mrs. Adams took her daughter's hand, and together the two went back to the beach where Peggy had seen the strangers. There was no one there, nor were there any footprints in the snow. Sometime later, the older woman realized that the unusual clothing Peggy described were British soldiers' uniforms from years ago. Living in seclusion, this little girl would never have seen soldiers, especially not soldiers from another country and another century. Given that children are vastly more likely to see paranormal phenomena than adults are, many believe Peggy Adams did see apparitions of long-dead British soldiers landing on Oak Island countless decades before. The child was absolutely firm in her conviction about what she'd seen and where. Even as an adult, she described what she'd witnessed that winter's day in exactly the same terms as she had the day it occurred.

People who had lived on the island for some time were not surprised by Peggy's sighting because, some years before that, a boy had also reported seeing men wearing red coats standing at that same spot. Even though more than two hundred years—and at least that many retellings—have passed, descriptions of the ghosts wearing red coats have remained amazingly consistent.

But Oak Island's ghost sightings aren't just restricted to children's visions. One day, a group of prospectors saw a large, old-fashioned rowboat approaching. The image was clear. There were eight men in the boat, four per side, each at an oar. The scene was so real to the men working on the dig that one of them called out a greeting. In response, the vision simply vanished as quickly as it had appeared. Perhaps those were the ghosts of the men who had buried the very cache the prospectors were after. If the phantoms had remained visible, would they have led the men to the treasure?

Other ghosts on the island have been more assertive. The esteemed Canadian folklorist Dr. Helen Creighton turned up two first-hand stories from people who'd had ghostly encounters on the island. In both cases, the spirits advised the treasure hunters that they were looking in the wrong place.

Today Oak Island is littered with pits and tunnels, yet no one has discovered anything of significant monetary value. The original oak forest is gone, and six men have died trying to find the buried treasure trove. The requirements of the curse have almost been met. Or have those requirements already been met? Six men have died while searching for the booty, but history seems to have forgotten those first two men who rowed their small boat out to Oak Island and simply vanished.

The treasure hunt continues to this day. Will the advantages of industrial and technological equipment finally outwit the curse and the ghosts? We'll have to wait and see.

Sable Island

Sable Island, Nova Scotia, is known as the Graveyard of the Atlantic, and the place comes by that moniker honestly. It is said that more than five hundred ships have been wrecked against the small outcropping of land's inhospitable coastline. Wild horses, seals, and birds are the island's only natural inhabitants.

But then there are inhabitants of the supernatural variety.

Some of the unlucky sailors who have been stranded on Sable Island for any length of time have seen the image of a woman sitting by a fire. They say she has a slight build and long dark hair. She is also soaked to the bone from head to toe and covered with sand.

If anyone calls to her, she extends her left hand, showing the witness a gruesome sight. The fourth finger on that hand is gone and blood pours from the stump that remains. Then, ever so slowly, the vision of the woman begins to walk away and out of sight. One man, Captain Torrens from the wrecked ship the *Francis*, followed her, calling out that he could help her. The image led him directly to a small lake at the centre of Sable Island—where she vanished from sight.

Some believed that the image was the ghost of a passenger who had been aboard the *Francis*.

Since Biblical times, tales of the thirteenth man have had great significance, and one of those stories involves Sable Island.

During the 1800s, whenever there was a shipwreck on the island, hardy crews of twelve men were dispatched in large rowboats to rescue any sailors who may have survived. Each man in the lifeboat worked a set of oars.

As they headed toward Sable Island, a dark shape would appear from the mist and move toward the rescuers and their lifeboat. Soon the shape took on the form of a human being, a man. Although no one ever saw the man board their small craft, they soon noticed that an extra oarsman was with them, helping them to fight through the churning seas. Once they had manoeuvred their boat close to Sable Island, the thirteenth man would silently vanish from sight.

Interestingly, all twelve of the sailors always recognized their helper because he had a hideous gash on his face—a wound that never healed.

In September of 1899, after a lighthouse on Sable Island caught fire and burned to the ground, cleanup crews found a small metal box that contained, among other items, a note dated September 10, 1857.

"Wind blowing S.E. Howard Murray is dead. He died at ten o'clock this morning. The gash on his right cheek festered and blood poisoning set in. Before he died he said he would come back; that he would always go out with the lifeboat in which he had rowed stroke oarsman for many years. I wonder if he will. We buried him this afternoon on the point."

It would seem that, even in death, Murray was a man of his word.

Spirits at the Bar

Scotsman Alexander Keith trained as a brewer in Northern England before immigrating to Canada in 1817. Three years later, he opened a brewery in Halifax, Nova Scotia, and some say his spirit has never left the business. Keith was well known for being fastidious about beer-making, and it's presumed that even death hasn't stopped him from closely overseeing the brewing process.

According to psychics, Alexander Keith's ghost is not the only one to haunt the building. Employees and customers alike have heard footsteps in empty hallways and the squeaking wheels of carts that were once used to move beer barrels from one spot to another.

The ghost of a sailor has been seen sitting at the bar chatting with a woman wearing a green and purple frock. The couple, looking out of place because of the dated clothing, is never seen for very long before it fades into a nearby wall and out of sight.

Forerunner

Barrachois was once a small farming community on Cape Breton Island, Nova Scotia, and home to an intriguing legend. Every evening for weeks, farm families would gather on a particular hill and watch as a phantom train moved slowly and silently along nonexistent train tracks. The witnesses watched in amazement as the locomotive pulling empty passenger cars came to a stop at a farmer's gate.

Like all good trains, this one ran on time. At seven in the evening, people would gather on the hill to see this amazing sight. When some folks decided to climb down the hill and take a closer look, their plan failed completely. They couldn't see the train at all, while those who stayed up on the hill were treated to a clear sighting of the engine pulling empty cars and stopping at the gate as it always did.

A month after this strange vision was first seen, a local farmer was hit by a train and killed. Neighbourhood folks all said they should have known the man was doomed. After all, it was his gate the phantom train stopped at.

His Soul Went Home

Some say that Cape Breton Island, Nova Scotia, is a land of coal miners and ghosts. The following snippet of a story bears witness to that theory.

On a warm summer afternoon many, many years ago, two Cape Breton women were chatting near their homes. Suddenly one of the women saw her husband, John, coming home from work and walking into their house. She broke off her conversation immediately and excused herself to check on her husband who, she presumed, must have taken ill because otherwise he would never have left the mine before his shift was over.

The other woman stayed outside to enjoy the fresh air for a time before heading back toward her house. Just as she did, she saw her own husband approaching. "Hello," he called out to her. "Sad news, I'm afraid. John was killed in an accident at the mine not more than half an hour ago."

The Lady in Blue

With its iconic lighthouse, Nova Scotia's picturesque Peggy's Cove is one of Canada's most recognizable locales. Less than 50 kilometres from Halifax, the quaint fishing village draws tourists from all over the world. A few of those visitors see more than the natural beauty. They also see a supernatural image: The Lady in Blue.

The wraith walks forlornly along the shoreline, the hem of her blue frock fluttering about her legs as the sea breezes blow around her. She looks down at the waves and then lifts her head and scans the vast expanse of water as though searching for someone or something. She's a heartbreaking image; her sorrow is so deep that it permeates the air around her. Anyone who sees the Lady in Blue feels her sadness.

Legend tells us that she is the ghost of a woman named Margaret who lived in the area back in the 1700s. Some say that the cove and the village are named after her, the name "Peggy" being a diminutive for Margaret. The young mother was the sole survivor of a shipwreck. She later died in the area, apparently of a broken heart. Her soul, though, has never stopped looking for her children, who were lost when the ship they were on wrecked against the rocks.

Occasionally the Lady in Blue appears aware of the living and actually tries to speak to a tourist who's come to admire the view. Any who have had this experience say that they haven't been able to understand what she was trying to say, that it seemed as if the grieving mother's words were swept away by a gust of wind. The people who've shared such an encounter all say that she seems to be reaching out across time, imploring them to help her.

Then the image in the blue dress slowly begins to fade away, leaving witnesses with only the beautiful scenery to look at.

PRINCE EDWARD ISLAND

The Legendary Bell Ringers

Every year, thousands of tourists flock to Canada's smallest province, Prince Edward Island, in search of anything and everything to do with a lovable fictional little red-haired girl. People may come for Anne of Green Gables, but they could certainly stay to enjoy the rich cache of ghostly lore that haunts the island. The story of Charlottetown's phantom bell ringers is a classic local ghost story.

The tale began on the morning of October 7, 1853, when many people in Charlottetown were awakened by the unexpected sound of bells ringing. A captain who lived in the city was one of those people. He struggled from his warm bed and made his way to the docks, presuming that a ship must have come in. But once he was at the harbour, he couldn't see or hear anything out of the ordinary. He even noted that a local steamship known as the *Fairy Queen* rested at anchor, just where it should, in anticipation of her voyage to Pictou, Nova Scotia, later that day.

Then the captain stood and listened as the same bells that had wakened him pealed once more. The sound was not coming from the dock, he realized, but from somewhere in town. He turned and walked away from the harbour and up toward town.

He hadn't gone far when he realized that it was the church bells that were ringing. *How odd*, he thought, and followed the sound to the Kirk of St. James. As the man arrived at the church grounds, he saw the filmy shapes of three women slip through the door of the building's bell tower. He may have thought that such a sight at that early hour was unusual, but he barely had time to consider the facts before the church's sexton joined him.

Together the two men climbed the steep stairs to the top of the bell tower. There they found the bell was still vibrating as if it had just been struck, even though there was no one else near it. The two men were puzzled, but there didn't seem to be anything for them to do, so they descended the stairs, and each went home to eat a well-deserved breakfast.

At noon that day, right on schedule, the *Fairy Queen* departed for Pictou with a complement of passengers and crew. The rest of the day proceeded like any other, until word reached Charlottetown that the *Fairy Queen* had hit rough waters and sunk. Seven passengers were lost. Three of those seven were women, members of the Kirk of St. James. It was their ghostly images that the captain had seen disappearing through the bell tower's door and for whom the bells had tolled.

That church building was replaced in 1878, but the congregants still treasure the story of the phantom bell ringers. Canada Post included the story in its third series of stamps depicting famous Canadian ghost stories.

Historian Ian Scott revealed that the church office still fields calls from people all over the world who are interested in the poignant story of the phantom bell ringers. He adds jokingly, "I always say that the bells have never really stopped ringing at the kirk. Now it's the telephone bells that ring."

The Haunted Light

The Northumberland Strait is picturesque from almost any vantage point, but a truly exceptional spot is the historic West Point Lighthouse near the community of O'Leary, Prince Edward Island. The old lighthouse still functions, but the light itself has been automated for more than fifty years.

Construction on the lighthouse was finished in the spring of 1876. Between then and 1963, when the light was automated, there were only two lighthouse keepers. William MacDonald first held the post and stayed on the job some fifty years. Incredibly, he never missed a day of work during all that time, not so much as one sick day. William's loyalty would have been a hard act to follow, but his replacement, Benjamin MacIsaac, also showed amazing dedication to his important job. He worked the light from 1925 until automation made the position redundant in 1963.

In the mid-1980s, work began on a project to turn the still-functioning lighthouse into a very special inn with a restaurant and a museum. Today, of course, no one works seven days a week like William did for all those years. In the early days of the renovations, a group of volunteers would stay at the tower while those in management took some well-deserved time off. One of those volunteers had an experience she'll never forget. She was preparing to lock up and leave for the evening when she climbed up the seventy-two steps to check the light. She found that all was well, and so she made her way back down the long staircase, turning off light switches as she went.

The woman got into her car with a sense of satisfaction at another successful volunteer shift, but as she turned her key in the ignition, something caught her eye. There was a light on in the tower. This was puzzling because she was sure she'd turned off every light in the building. Clearly, though, she'd missed one light switch on her final round.

She went back into the tower, turned off the offending light, and hurried back to her car. She hadn't heard or seen anything unusual during the hours she'd been inside, so she wasn't concerned about a possible intruder, but she was a bit perplexed and anxious to get on her way home. She started her car and glanced back at the lighthouse again. The same light she had just turned off was shining brightly again. This time she didn't dare go back inside. She'd heard tales that the lighthouse was haunted, and she had no desire to encounter a presence, especially in the evening when she was alone. She decided that if the ghost wanted a light turned on, then it was fine by her.

Some months later during the refurbishing process, a group of people met in the lighthouse to review the builder's drawings. These people were all familiar with the lighthouse and knew they had to shut down all the electricity except, of course, the power to the rotating beacon that had signalled to ships for nearly a hundred years. The group members worked as a team to fulfill their obligations and then got ready to leave for the evening—or so they thought. They were no sooner at their cars than they realized they'd left the drawings inside. No one particularly wanted to go back inside, especially not alone, but one man took a flashlight from his vehicle and did just that. He rolled up the papers and scanned the flashlight around the room one last time. All was as it should be, so he let himself out into the parking lot again, and the small convoy of cars headed toward town.

They hadn't gone very far when a man at the side of the road flagged them down. He told the volunteers that a neighbour of his was distraught; he was afraid the person might go to the lighthouse and try to jump to certain death. With a human life at stake, the volunteers knew they needed to go back to the tower and assure themselves that the building was, in fact, locked and secure.

When they got back to the site, they were horrified to see that a light was turned on. They hurried toward the door, afraid that the distressed person had somehow broken in. But the door was locked. Then they checked the electrical panel. It too was turned off.

Just then, the man who'd stopped them on the road arrived to tell them that his neighbour was back at home and all was well.

This left the group with only one concern: How had the light come on in that room when there was no power to the switch?

By now many folks are convinced that, even in death, one of the long-deceased dedicated lighthouse keepers has not left his post. Most people think the ghost is William MacDonald, the keeper who never missed a day of work. Perhaps his amazing work ethic has carried through to the afterlife. If so, then perhaps William is also the one who makes his ethereal presence known occasionally in the form of inexplicable cold spots scattered about the tower and lights turning on and off.

There are even rumours that pirates buried chests of precious jewels near the lighthouse centuries ago. With treasure, a resident ghost, and a chance to see the fiery phantom ship, the lighthouse could be the ultimate all-inclusive vacation destination!

Kellow's Hollow

By the mid-1700s, immigrants from Europe and the British Isles had begun settling in the beautiful area that would become known as Prince Edward Island. The Connaway family was among those early settlers. Jack Connaway and his brother Michael were popular young men who lived and worked on a farm in a small community just west of Charlottetown.

Late one cold November evening after he had been socializing at the local pub, Jack said goodbye to his friends, climbed aboard his trusty mare, and headed for home. He'd only gone as far as Kellow's Hollow, where a bridge spanned a small stream, when his horse became nervous. Jack patted the mare's neck and spoke reassuringly to her—as reassuringly as he could, that is, because he was well aware of the local legends. Jack had even heard talk that many ghosts haunted both the bridge and the huge pine tree nearby.

Rumour had it that a man had hanged himself from that tree, and since then, the enormous pine had become home to many wandering spirits. It was even thought that the bridge itself was jinxed. Most people would go well out of their way to avoid crossing its short span under the glow of a full moon.

But that night, Jack was feeling far too brave to bother worrying about any such ridiculous superstitions, so he urged his horse on. But the normally obedient steed resisted. With a pat to her flank and a kindly, "easy girl, just go easy," he coaxed her on. But by now she had come to a stop and would not move, so once more he coaxed, "easy girl, just go easy." The horse took just one tentative step forward when an ear-piercing wail came from the stream below. The horse reared up, throwing Jack onto the bridge below, killing him instantly. From a distance, James Kellow had watched the deadly scenario unfold. He raced to Jack's side, but there was nothing he could do.

The community honoured Jack with a fitting funeral, and then most of the folks moved on. But Michael, Jack's brother, still grieved deeply.

One beautiful night when the Hollow was bathed in the glow of a full moon, Michael rode his horse toward the bridge where his brother had died. He stopped for a moment to pay his respects to Jack. Perhaps he even thought of changing his route in order to avoid crossing that bridge, but he needed to get home quickly and any other route would take him far out of his way.

He stroked his horse's neck and ordered, "go girl," but the animal neighed and pawed at the ground, thrusting her head back in protest. Michael looked around to see what the horse was reacting to and could barely believe his eyes. The pine tree beside the bridge was ablaze with dancing lights of all different colours. He gasped, and as he did, the coloured lights fell to the ground.

Just then he heard another horse galloping toward him. Michael smiled with relief. There would be a man on that horse, and Michael badly needed the company of another human being right then. But when he looked around, he couldn't see either horse or rider. How could that be? The hoofbeats were getting louder, closer to him, but there was nothing to see. Then Michael felt a blast of air as an invisible horse and rider galloped past him—so close that he could hear his brother's voice say, "Easy girl, go easy."

Michael recognized that voice. That was Jack's voice, and that was how his brother had always spoken to his horse.

"Jack?" Michael called. His brother's apparition materialized before his eyes. But Jack wasn't alone. He was surrounded by dozens of ghosts, as many ghosts as there had been lights on that pine tree just moments before. Michael watched in terror as the gathering of ghosts made its way toward the bridge, floating effortlessly. None of them, not even Jack, seemed aware of Michael's presence.

Sometime later, the community decided that Kellow's Hollow would be the perfect spot on which to build a church, so the enormous pine tree was cut down. It's not known whether the wood was used in any of the church's furnishings, but people still tend to avoid that area during a full moon. They say the shrieks and moans wafting up from the ground just make a person uneasy.

The Haunted Stage

The MacKenzie Theatre, or the "Mack" as it is fondly known, is located in the heart of Charlottetown, Prince Edward Island. The theatre opened in 1930 as the Capital Theatre, a movie house. Then in the mid-1970s, the Mack was converted to a stage theatre. The auditorium is an intimate space, seating two hundred people with the rehearsal area, the green room, and the dressing rooms efficiently tucked underneath the stage.

Over the years, Reg "Dutch" Thompson worked at various tasks in the theatre. Depending on the performance being staged, he was responsible for lighting, scenery, or props, sometimes all three. When he was busy during a performance, Dutch often recorded a radio show to enjoy when he'd finished work. Given that paranormal presences seem to be drawn to electrical or electronic devices, his plan did not always work out well. Sometimes the volume on the radio would gradually get louder and louder until it was loud enough that the stage manager complained. All of this while no one was in the room where the radio's volume had been set to a mere whisper. And that was when Dutch knew that he was not only working with a group of talented and dedicated individuals, he was also working with a very mischievous ghost.

On days when there was a matinee performance as well as one in the evening, the actors and musicians usually stayed at the theatre between shows and relaxed in the green room below the stage. Dutch, however, almost always left the building. He would lock the theatre before leaving, knowing that, if there was a fire, there were crash bars on all the doors so no one's safety would be jeopardized.

When Dutch returned for the later performance, those who were new to the Mack would often ask him if he had been walking around on the stage. They would tell him they could hear footfalls across the wooden boards. Some of those folks would go upstairs to see who had come into the theatre. Veterans didn't bother. They knew that the stage would be empty—of a visible presence anyway.

Years ago, an actor relaxing in the green room overheard what he described as party noises coming from another part of the theatre. He was surprised because he'd thought he was alone in the building. Not wanting to miss out on the fun, he searched the theatre and found that he was, indeed, the only person inside. Even so, he knew for certain what he'd heard. After that, the actor wasn't as keen on staying alone in the Mack. Others have been sure they saw someone walking across the catwalk above the stage, but when they looked again they realized there was no one there.

Many people who work or live with a ghost give the presence a name, and those at the Mack were no exception. They named their phantom Charlie. Considerately, the staff tried to keep the existence of the resident wraith a secret from the newcomers. If there happened to be supernatural activity going on and rookies were present, the seasoned staff would use the ghost's name as a code. One of them might say, "Charlie's been here recently." Then the person he was speaking too would simply reply, "We'll talk about that later."

The MacKenzie Theatre staged the popular musical *A Closer Walk with Patsy Cline*, and the run was a great success. Part of the staging included a mock-up of an old-fashioned radio station sound booth with an actor dressed as an old-time reporter, including a fedora hat complete with a press pass and a pencil jammed into the hatband.

Time and time again, just as the actor was about to make his entrance, the pencil would fly from the hatband and land on the floor. Needless to say, the man was annoyed. To assure the frustrated actor that none of his colleagues were playing tricks on him, Dutch explained the presence of the theatre's ghost.

One season, a new company took over managing the theatre's bar, and the boss insisted that all the locks be changed in the bar area so that there was only one key, which she would keep with her at all times. Then she stored the bottles of liquor in a locked cabinet inside the bar.

While the liquor service was being looked after in a new manner, all the details surrounding the life of the theatre and the theatrical workers continued unchanged. This meant that all the staff members brought their own coffee mugs into work. The stage manager took on the chore of washing all the mugs at the end of the day. Soon he noticed that the number of cups was dwindling. He didn't want clutter in an already tight space, so he asked everyone to find their mugs and bring them to the sink. The others tried to oblige, but no one could find any cups.

A few days later, the new bar manager approached Dutch. It was clear by her demeanour that she was annoyed. When he asked what the problem was, she told him that she didn't appreciate his sense of humour. The man was stunned. He couldn't imagine what she was referring to until she spoke again, demanding that he remove all the staff's cups from inside her locked bar.

Dutch looked at her incredulously until she opened the bar door. There, neatly stacked along with the rum and vodka, were more than a dozen freshly washed coffee mugs. They were the missing coffee mugs.

Understandably, Dutch was not about to accept blame for the prank when he was completely innocent. After the show that night, he had everyone who worked in the theatre meet at the bar area. Then he asked if anyone knew anything about the coffee mugs. They all shook their heads. Everyone left the meeting puzzled but with cup in hand and resolved to keep better track of the possessions they brought to work. Their resolutions weren't helpful though because one by one the mugs disappeared again only to turn up in the locked bar once more. The strange situation continued throughout the run of *A Closer Walk with Patsy Cline* and the mystery was never solved. The ghostly antics, however, continued.

In October, the Mack staged the play *Dracula*. The production required hiring new employees who had never been in the building before. Charlie must have liked all the new faces because he made himself visible and even audible. Dutch resigned himself to the likelihood that this was going to be a hauntingly busy season, and the new hires gained more experience in a theatre than they'd counted on.

One evening two employees from the bar were relaxing with a drink after the theatre was empty and their work was done. They heard voices in the hallway and went out to see who had come back into the locked building, but there was no one anywhere to be seen. Another time the pair heard footsteps walking across the empty stage, and sometimes they heard such loud noises that they feared a burglar had broken in. Dutch always reassured them that they had merely encountered Charlie the ghost.

It's thought that Charlie is the spirit of a man who died in a fire that ravaged an entire block of downtown Charlottetown in the 1940s. His soul has apparently been a presence in the MacKenzie Theatre ever since.

NEW BRUNSWICK

The Voice

Not all ghosts are visual images. Some spirits come to us as mere whiffs of fragrance or, as in the story that follows, simply a sound.

The year was 1889. The place was St. Martins, New Brunswick. Young Jack Dyer had been hired to help crew a ship christened the *Union*. Dyer loved the sea and looked forward to many adventures aboard the freighter, and like most of us, Jack worked to earn money. When the opportunity came up to earn a little extra cash, he jumped at the chance—especially since the assignment seemed to be an easy one.

The *Union*'s captain and the other crew members all wanted to go ashore for a night, but someone needed to stay aboard the ship. Before long, the group had negotiated an arrangement, and everyone was happy. Jack would have a little extra in his pay packet, and the other men could enjoy some shore leave.

Because there was little to do aboard the docked vessel, Jack decided to go to bed early, but just before he did, he made one final check of the vessel. All was secure and quiet; the man fell into his bunk and was asleep in no time.

Not long after, Jack Dyer woke up with a start. He sat straight up in bed, sure that he had heard someone call out his name. Worse, the voice warned him to leave the ship immediately. Although he was badly frightened, Jack knew he was responsible for finding the trespasser who had come on the boat. Despite a thorough search of a vessel he knew well, Jack could not find anyone on board, nor could he find anything unusual anywhere in the ship. Relieved, he returned to his bed where, after tossing and turning for a few minutes, he fell back asleep.

Just as he drifted off, the voice came again. "Jack Dyer, you must leave this ship now." Even more terrified this time, Jack sat shivering in bed, the covers pulled up around him, trying to get up the courage to do what he knew he had to do: check again for an intruder.

Moments later, Jack rose from his warm, secure bunk and once again inspected the ship, this time even more carefully. He found no possible source for the mysterious voice. Badly confused and frightened, he returned to his bed, but he knew falling asleep would be impossible.

As he lay awake, pleading silently and futilely for morning to come quickly, he heard the voice again. "Jack Dyer, you must leave this ship now."

By daybreak, Dyer had had enough. The frightened man had no idea what or who could have spoken to him, he just knew for certain that he would never set sail on that vessel again. He was packed and ready to leave the ship as soon as his captain returned.

Although the captain of the *Union* tried very hard to change his sailor's mind, Dyer left. The captain knew that a replacement worker would have to be found before they could set out again. There were dozens of other young men on the docks who wanted adventure, so he had no trouble hiring someone. The *Union*, her core senior crew, and one new man sailed out of the port by noon.

The captain could tell right away that this trip was not going to be a fast one. There was almost no wind, and any progress the ship made was because of the tide. Once well out into the Bay of Fundy, the wind died down completely. The *Union* and dozens of other ships were completely becalmed.

As experienced sailors, those stranded on the still waters of the bay simply set about swabbing the decks and shining the brass on their ships, waiting for the wind to pick up. For the *Union*, however, that time really never did come. As she rested on the water's calm surface, the ship overturned. The captain and one crew member were rescued. The man who took Jack Dyer's place was among those whose bodies were never recovered.

It would seem that heeding the phantom voice had saved Jack Dyer's life.

If this were a fictional ghost story, all the loose ends would be tied up. A true ghost story such as this can have a ragged feel to it and leave us wanting more, wondering why Jack was chosen to survive that day when others died. Did he go on to accomplish something meaningful for humankind? We can hope so, but we'll never know for certain.

The Algonquin

In the late 1800s, Canada's economy was booming, and enormous elegant hotels were being built right across the country. The Algonquin Resort in St. Andrews-by-the-Sea, New Brunswick, was one of those. Financed by a consortium of American investors, the hotel's first advertising campaign capitalized on the bracing seaside climate. Brochures from that era extolled the health benefits of a vacation at the seaside and proclaimed, "no hay fever here." Other advertising described the hotel as "an incomparable resting place and retreat from the cares of business and the heat and dust and bustle of the city."

Of course, all of these luxurious advantages came at a price, with rooms costing as much as three to five dollars a day.

A few years later, the resort opened its world-class golf course. According to the Algonquin's website, the course "quickly became one of the hottest attractions" in the quaint little town of St. Andrews.

In 1924, a fire razed the hotel, and the Algonquin had to be almost completely rebuilt. Since then, the elegant and sprawling resort has been kept up to date with additional renovations but maintains its original charm—and an assortment of ethereal presences.

One of the most intriguing ghost stories comes from a family that was helped by a bellman who chatted with the guests as he carried their bags, offering a detailed history of both the hotel and the town of St. Andrews-by-the-Sea. The bellman set the suitcases in the family's room. Just as the father reached into his wallet to offer a tip, the bellman vanished without a trace.

The Algonquin Resort must be an enjoyable place to work because in addition to the phantom bellman, there is also the spirit of a night watchman. He is sometimes heard making his rounds with an enormous ring of keys jingling at his side—for eternity.

It is thought that room 473 is haunted by the cries of a jilted bride. Oddly, small objects have been known to go missing temporarily from that floor. Could there be a connection? No one seems to know.

Two rooms on the third floor, numbers 308 and 373, are also thought to be haunted, and people have seen phantom lights and the image of a woman in the building's tower. It's clear that neither the lights nor the woman are of this life because the entrance to the tower has been closed off for years. The ghosts of children playing have also been reported, as well as the silhouette of a little boy.

One of the eeriest tales comes from the second floor: doorknobs have been seen turning when no one is near them.

There is also the apparition of an older woman who has been known to rearrange furniture in the guest rooms. Perhaps this was the spectre that visited a student named Christine one summer night when she worked at the hotel.

Christine explained that, late in July, she and her five roommates were asleep in their dorm when something woke her up. She looked toward the doorway and saw a shape moving toward her until it was close enough that she could see that it was a woman wearing gloves, a hat, and an old-fashioned dress.

Presuming that a hotel guest had somehow lost her way, Christine called out quietly, asking if she could help the seemingly lost soul. There was no answer, but by now Christine could sense the woman's confusion and asked again if she could help, this time a bit louder. The presence still didn't reply, but one of the other girls in the dorm woke up and asked what was going on. With that the figure disappeared as mysteriously as it had appeared.

The two girls who had been awoken soon drifted off to sleep again, but in the morning Christine was still bothered by the encounter. She tried to talk to her co-workers about the sighting, but when they looked at her askance, she dropped the subject and did her best to forget the incident.

Many years later, Christine read the book *The Ghost of Flight 401* by John G. Fuller, which describes ghosts appearing in a certain type of aircraft. That was when she finally realized she had seen a ghost that night.

Researchers into the paranormal would likely define the visitation as a temporal anomaly, a spirit reaching out from the past. For Christine, the entire summer working at the Algonquin was a time of her life she'll remember fondly.

As for the Algonquin Resort's official stance on the hauntings? They are good sports and take a light-hearted approach to the hotel's haunted status—there are even ghost tours on offer.

Apparition on Staff

The palatial old Capitol Theatre in Moncton, New Brunswick, is a landmark on Main Street. The auditorium seats eight hundred. Or perhaps that should be eight hundred and one.

The theatre first opened in 1920 as a venue for vaudeville performances, but early in 1926, a devastating fire broke out and ravaged the building. Alexander Lindsay, fondly known as "Sandy," was one of the volunteer firefighters who responded to the alarm. Sadly, he was in the basement of the building when the stage collapsed, killing him instantly.

Sandy's spirit, however, has never left the theatre where he died. His image has been seen in the balcony happily floating just above the floor. On the main floor, an empty seat will periodically squeak as though an invisible audience member is adjusting, trying to get comfortable.

The firefighter's spirit is so accepted at the theatre that virtually everyone working there has at least sensed Sandy. His name is even listed on the Capitol's masthead, with the title "Resident Ghost." With appreciation like that, it's safe to say that heroic Alexander Lindsay will be haunting that house for years to come.

Girl's Grave

If you travel from the Capitol Theatre on Moncton's Main Street to Gorge Road, you will come to the site of a peculiar landmark. It's nothing grand, just an ordinary slab of concrete, but there is nothing ordinary about the ghost story that accompanies that odd spot. Legend has it that this chunk of cement covers the grave of a teenage girl named Rebecca Lutes who died in 1876 at the young age of sixteen. There was nothing natural about Rebecca's death, and if you believe those who put her to death, her life wasn't natural either.

Rebecca's parents had no doubt heard that farmland was plentiful in New Brunswick, and they wanted to take advantage. Unfortunately, their timing was not good. A severe drought was killing crops almost as soon as they were planted. Worse, the lack of moisture meant that the least spark of a flame sent fires spreading, virtually unchecked, throughout the area. Then, on top of those natural disasters, seemingly supernatural events made life even more frightening. Livestock began to disappear for no discernable reason.

Worse, frightening rumours began to circulate. There were eerie and inexplicable lights flitting about on paths, people said, and even the possibility that witchcraft was being practiced in the forest. The terrified farmers needed an explanation, and poor young Rebecca became a scapegoat. Neighbours proclaimed her to be a witch, saying that her Wiccan practices were to blame for all their troubles. They reasoned that there was nothing to be done except put the girl to death. And so sixteen-year-old Rebecca Lutes was hanged from a tall poplar tree.

Once the child had breathed her last, the locals cut her body down and buried her face down, in case there was any life left in her to scratch her way out of her grave. They reasoned that if that happened and she was face down, she'd reach Hell rather than return to the desperate farming community. Then, for extra insurance, they sealed the area over her coffin with concrete. What they didn't predict was the appearance of Rebecca's ghost.

The girl's spirit haunted the area near her grave long past the time when anyone involved with her killing had gone to his or her final reward—whatever that might have been. But even that was not enough to settle Rebecca's restless spirit. Perhaps to maintain the theory that Rebecca had been evil and to blame for all the farmers' problems, a story grew that her ghost had been seen peering into an old church window accompanied by a black cat, as folklore dictates is customary for witches. Others say they've seen a phantom black cat roaming near Rebecca's gravesite. They know the animal isn't just someone's pet out exploring the neighbourhood because this cat disappears from sight in the blink of an eye.

Given its ghoulish history, it shouldn't be much of a surprise that visiting Rebecca's gravesite at midnight is a rite of passage for local youth. That concrete slab is still an area prone to odd mists and lights, and the air around it is always unnaturally cold.

The Dungarvon Whooper

Some ghost stories become woven into the culture of their setting and that is certainly the case of the legend of the Dungarvon Whooper.

Back in the 1860s, when Ireland's deadly potato famine wreaked havoc across the land, those who were able to often escaped to the New World. Usually they came with nothing more than the clothes on their backs, but at least one young man was fortunate enough to have brought a stash of money with him. Most retellings of this story refer to the lad as Ryan. Some say his full name was Peter Ryan. Be that as it may, the boy made his way to a lumber camp near the Miramichi River in New Brunswick, where he offered his services as a cook.

The crew of lumberjacks took to Ryan right away because, by all accounts, he was an excellent cook as well as outgoing, friendly, and trusting, perhaps too trusting. He often showed off the money belt that he kept strapped around his waist. Each morning the men would head into the forest knowing that, by lunchtime, they would hear Ryan's distinctive whooping call, letting them know their noon meal was ready.

One frigid winter's day, the crew's foreman announced that he was staying behind at the camp to attend to paperwork. The men nodded, picked up their tools, and headed out for a morning's work. By the time the sun was high in the clear sky and their stomachs were rumbling with hunger, they realized that they had not heard Ryan's characteristic whoop. They set down their axes and made their way back to the cookhouse. Much to their surprise, the makeshift structure was deserted.

Ryan was not there, nor was there any food ready for them. They searched for the boss and found him in his cabin. He told them there would be no hot lunch because, sadly, the popular young cook had taken sick and died that morning.

The crew was devastated to lose its co-worker that way, but there wasn't much they could do. It was too cold to even dig a proper grave for the deceased. That night the men all said a prayer for their friend as they bedded down to sleep. Their heads had no sooner hit the pillow than they were startled by the sound of whooping and hollering coming from the porch of the cookhouse.

The bravest man went to see what had caused the familiar cry, but all he saw was Ryan's dead body lying in the snow. The dreadful cries echoed through the entire night. By morning the men were exhausted, but they knew what they had to do. They dug a shallow grave and buried the corpse under the snow. Perhaps that would settle the young man's spirit. But it didn't. The whoops continued until the terrified lumberjacks fled from the camp into the nearby town.

The crew's foreman was never seen again, but the same cannot be said for the young lad from Ireland who came to Canada with the hope of making a good life for himself.

Some say they have seen his transparent apparition rise from the ground where the men placed his body, but most have just heard Ryan's unusual call echoing through the forest. Word of the dreadful sounds spread throughout the community. People wondered if his soul was trying to call attention to his wrongful death. They set out to find the foreman, but he had vanished. Soon it was presumed that their former boss was a murderer.

But that opinion was not enough to lay the hollering banshee to rest. No woodsman would go near that part of the forest. One declared, "You can't imagine the devastating impact of the wild yells. Stout-hearted men were reduced to numbed, unreasoning, panicky creatures with only one overwhelming impulse: to flee."

A few say the whole story was concocted by woodsmen who didn't want to work, but if that was the case then why, asked Frank Estey of Sevogle, is it "that never a brush has growed in half an acre around the grave?"

Decades later, in an attempt to bring peace to the haunted area, a local priest named Father Edward S. Murdoch trekked into the forest and blessed the place where Ryan had been killed. Some say the ritual was effective, others such as New Brunswick folklorist Stuart Trueman, maintain the ghostly cries continued.

Even horses used to haul logs would shy away from the young man's gravesite. Then, when a steam train replaced the horse-and-wagon method of getting the logs to market, the train was nicknamed the "Dungarvon Whooper" because the sound of its whistle sounded like the ghost's cry.

That train hasn't run since the 1960s, but a poem, a play, and a folk song keep the ghostly legend of the Dungarvon Whooper alive today.

Murder Most Foul

Fredericton, New Brunswick, is a very pretty city—with at least one really ugly ghost story.

The tragedy began in January 1949. "Silver" Burgoyne, a young husband and father, was a man with the future on his mind. He had recently bought a business, the Rideout Taxi Company. In order to make his company stand out from other taxi companies, Burgoyne's cabs weren't just run-of-the-mill cars but classier upscale models, and he kept them meticulously clean. No doubt he hoped to appeal to a better segment of the taxi-taking population, but those hopes proved to be wrong—tragically wrong.

Just after eight o'clock on the evening of January 7, 1949, Silver thought he was through work for the day. He'd already enjoyed dinner at home with his wife, two daughters, and one young son. But when a call came to pick up two men at the local legion hall, he decided to take the trip. He assured his wife that he wouldn't be gone long. His family never saw him alive again.

The young Hamilton brothers, George and Rufus, were waiting outside the legion hall when they saw Silver's cab pull up to the curb. Burgoyne must have known immediately that the two were very intoxicated.

Mrs. Burgoyne wasn't overly concerned when her husband was later getting home than he had predicted. Perhaps the fare from the legion had taken him out of town. By midnight, though, she was sick with worry. No trip should have taken her husband that long.

First thing Saturday morning, she called the police.

It was Monday when the police located the classy Ford that Burgoyne had been so pleased to call his own. The cab had been abandoned at the side of the road in an area on the outskirts of Fredericton known as Barkers Point.

When the constable forced open the car's trunk, he made a gruesome discovery. There, wrapped in a blanket, was Norman Phillip Burgoyne's bloodied body. His skull had been beaten with a hammer.

The police lost little time in locating the murderers. By interviewing the brothers separately, they were able to build solid cases against both George and Rufus Hamilton. It seemed the brothers had been attracted to Burgoyne's high-end car, but not for the reason the cab owner had hoped. The Hamiltons presumed that Burgoyne was rich, and that made him a prime target. They had made off with Norman's Rolex watch and two hundred dollars in cash. They claimed they had not intended to kill the driver, but that brought them little leniency in the court system. In July of that year, both George and Rufus were sentenced to death and hanged.

The spirit of the brutally murdered cab driver seems to have immediately gone on to its eternal rest.

But the souls of the "Hammer brothers," as the pair came to be called, have not allowed themselves to be forgotten. Rufus and George's ghosts are always seen together, as they were in life and death. People have seen them skulking through back alleys and have watched them until their supernatural images simply vanish from sight.

The ghostly brothers' scariest appearances are at the roadside near the murder scene. That stretch of road leads to the area of the city where the Hamiltons were born and raised. It is said that their apparitions are turned toward oncoming cars and slowly walking backward, each with their right arm out and thumb up, hitchhiking back home. No one ever stops, or even slows down, when they see George and Rufus because everyone in the area knows who they were in life, and no one has any desire to find out if they've become any better in their afterlife.

Rufus and George were only a year apart in age, so their backgrounds were identical—and complex. They viewed Burgoyne as a rich white man, which they were not. George and Rufus were of combined Micmac and African Canadian ancestry and had lived in abject poverty with violent, abusive, and neglectful parents.

George Elliott Clarke is a multi-award-winning writer who is also a descendant of the Hamilton brothers. Although Clarke was born more than ten years after George and Rufus were executed, he developed an intense interest in their lives and what had driven them to commit their heinous crime. Clarke has preserved the lives and deaths of the Hamilton brothers in a novel and a book of poetry. Academic papers have also been written about the murder and the murderers.

It's highly unlikely that any of those writings would appeal to the ghosts of George and Rufus Hamilton.

Intruders

Some people, and even some families, seem more likely to have a ghostly encounter than others. This was certainly the situation for a New Brunswick family we will call the Lawsons.

Bob Lawson recalled an especially stressful time for his family during World War II, the winter of 1942 to be exact. "My brother Gerry, a mechanic, was in the Air Force. He and another man were on mercy flights in the north with a bush pilot named Al. They were on a mission to deliver medicine to some northern people when their plane went down and they were lost for thirteen days."

During this time of terrible worry, the family tried to keep going as best they could. Mrs. Lawson, for instance, kept up with her household responsibilities.

"My mother had waxed the floors, and it was snowing, so she put newspapers over them. One Saturday night about midnight, we heard the front door open. We could hear the squeaking of the frosted hinges, and then we heard someone stomp his feet on the floor, as if to bang the snow off his boots. Then we heard three heavy knocks at the door. My sister and my father went downstairs to see who had come in.

"There was absolutely nobody there, nor was there a drop of water on the newspapers. The two of them looked all through the house. They went out and looked on the front porch and there was about a foot of snow, but no footprints in the snow. I remember my mother saying, 'That's Gerry asking for prayers, probably dead and asking for prayers.'"

The following morning, the family received a phone call from the Air Force base telling them that the flight crew had survived the plane crash and that rescuers were on their way to bring the three men out.

The news wiped away the sorrow the family had felt after hearing the ghostly footsteps throughout that eerie snowy night. They decided to invite friends and relatives over to celebrate the good news. As the group toasted Gerry's good fortune, there was a knock at the door. The parish priest stood in the doorway and asked if they were related to a particular man who had died on Saturday night.

Bob explained that the dead man had been a troubled soul whom his mother had tried to help many times. It took a while before the family was able to make sense of what had happened. The phantom footsteps that they'd attributed to Gerry's soul passing by had, in fact, been those of the family friend.

The ironies of life—and of the afterlife—can be poignant.

Many years later, that same house was the scene of a very similar paranormal event. Bob's daughter, Angie, was an adult by then. She recalled that she and her husband were living with her parents in rural New Brunswick when one night, well past midnight when everyone in the house was asleep, they heard someone walking on the porch.

Slowly and quietly, Angie's brother went down the stairs to see who it was, but by the time he got there the sounds had stopped, and there was no sign that anyone had been near the house. Sensibly, the family decided to go back to bed, but their rest was short-lived because a few minutes later they heard the footsteps. Angie, her brother, and her husband all went downstairs this time, but again there was no one there.

"Again," Angie recalled, "we all went back to bed."

But their peace was disrupted for a third time.

The next morning at breakfast, they discussed the strange sounds from the night before and wondered what the source might be. Later that day, the family received a sad answer. "My husband, Chris, heard about an accident that happened about a thirty-minute drive from where we were. A man driving a small car in the early morning, approximately 1:30 a.m., crossed the centre line on the road and was hit head-on by an oncoming truck."

It was later determined that the car's driver died instantly.

Angie continued, "That man was a good friend of my husband's family. They say the spirit tries to find someone close to them. In this case that 'someone' was my husband. Those footsteps we heard that night sounded like the way that man walked. A sluggish walk with heavy boots, which is exactly what it sounded like when he walked."

They concluded that the spirit of her husband's friend had passed close by them on his way to the great beyond.

Phantom Ships

Canada's vast coastlines are home to some amazing ghost stories and a veritable fleet of phantom ships. It's hard to say which coast has the most dramatic sea stories, but the following tales are certainly some of the most enduring and remarkable of maritime ghost lore.

The Northumberland Strait separates Prince Edward Island from Nova Scotia and New Brunswick. While locals might take this gorgeous bit of geography for granted, visitors come from all over the world to enjoy the beautiful views and sandy beaches. There's one sight, however, that even residents don't take lightly: the image of a fiery schooner that's been plying the strait since the 1800s.

Over the years, hundreds of people have looked out across the water at an old, three-masted schooner sailing toward the harbour at Charlottetown. Some have even heard her cannons booming. She's most commonly seen in the autumn, often just before a storm, but people have seen her in all seasons. The apparition is a magnificent sight, so clear and convincing that witnesses usually assume they're seeing a carefully crafted reproduction of an old sailing ship. As the vessel sails closer to land, witnesses are excited to see sailors in old-fashioned clothing climbing on the riggings while other men work on the deck.

Then, when the image comes closer still, those on the shore are shocked to see that the ship is fully engulfed in flames.

This apparition is no trick of the light. The burning ship once caused dockworkers to drop their chores and hurry out in rowboats to try and rescue the imperilled crew. The rescuers nearly reached the distressed schooner when a bank of fog rolled in and engulfed it. Moments later the dark cloud vapourized. The would-be rescuers were left to stare at—nothing. The burning ship was no longer there.

A similar sighting occurred on a summer's day. Beachgoers were enjoying their afternoon when a woman noticed something odd coming into view on the horizon. Soon the small, dark shape had everyone's attention. Dozens of people watched in amazement as the phantom ship appeared. As the ship sailed closer to the beach, the swimmers were horrified to see that the vessel was engulfed in a raging inferno. The image came closer and closer until the witnesses could see sailors on board frantically trying to extinguish the fires that burned on the ship's deck. Then, as the people on shore began to run for help, a cloud of fog formed. Moments later the fog cleared; the burning ship was nowhere to be seen.

A group of young men in Charlottetown near Victoria Harbour looked out across the water. They stood mesmerized by the sight before them: the Northumberland Strait's flaming ship. When retelling their adventure, all four always noted that although the flames on board were raging, the ship was never consumed by the fire.

Some think the burning ship is the ghost of a privateer schooner called the *Young Teazer*. During the War of 1812, she and her crew were scavenging in the waters around Canada's Maritimes provinces when a much larger and better-armed ship threatened her. It's said that at least one of the *Young Teazer*'s crew members could not stand the humiliation of being taken down and set his own ship on fire. The mammoth explosion that resulted killed many men and severely burned others.

There are those who say that the inferno still burns today, on some other plane of existence. Those who make that claim have seen the ghost ship ablaze.

And, as if seeing a flaming wreck from beyond would not be disturbing enough, a sighting of the *Teazer* has long been taken as a sign that a severe storm is imminent.

The *Teazer* is especially interesting because, while several people might be gathered at the same spot on the shoreline, some will see the image clearly and others not at all. Perhaps not everyone is equally blessed, or cursed, with the ability to detect such ghostly resonation from the past.

Of course, those who know historic ships well are able to identify the spectre they're seeing with certainty. Those with less knowledge might easily mistake other phantoms on the bay for the ghostly privateer. For instance, more than a hundred years after the *Teazer* went down, an oil tanker caught fire and sank in the same area. This deadly blaze has also been seen many times over the years. When it is replayed, it has sometimes been misidentified as a sighting of the *Teazer*.

Other maritime apparitions that continue to play out as some sort of double exposure—a bygone era superimposed on the present—seem to be more aggressive.

Many years ago, Joseph Hyson, a lifelong resident of the Maritimes, explained that old-fashioned ships and crews have followed modern-day sailors, sometimes for hours and even right to shore. There were other instances reported by sailors who were so curious about a spectre they'd spotted that they rowed out to meet the ghostly vessel—only to have the ship disappear before their eyes.

Time and time again, these phantom ships stay their course straight for shore, leading those who see them to believe they've seen the ghosts of long-dead pirates intent on protecting their buried treasure.

The late author and folklorist Dr. Helen Creighton collected first-hand accounts from long-time residents of the Mahone Bay area indicating that some sightings of a flaming rig are misidentified as the *Young Teazer*. An examination of the area's history reveals enough trauma to leave many scars on the surrounding psychic landscape. Storms have always been a risk to sailors, and pirates were also a very real and lethal threat in the 1800s. It would seem that the ghosts of these seafaring thieves have remained behind to give us the occasional history lesson.

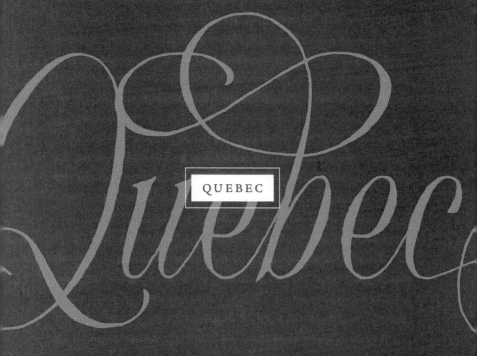

QUEBEC

Historical Haunt

In 1877, William Kirby published a novel called *The Golden Dog*. The plot is grim but romantic, set against actual historic events. Amazingly, more than a hundred and thirty years later, that book, in a somewhat abridged form, is still in print. It offers a raw and colourful glimpse into life in Quebec City during the mid-1700s. *The Golden Dog* also provides a dramatic description of a ghost who, legend has it, still haunts the original section of that city.

The sight of this haggard spectre is not one that any witness could readily dismiss. In life, Marie-Josephte La Corriveau proudly declared that she was a witch. If her claim was true, then her actions proved that she was a vicious one. La Corriveau had been suspected of being involved in a murder by poisoning before eventually being convicted of a second murder—that of her husband. According to Canadian historian Frank Anderson, she killed her husband "by pouring molten lead into his ear while he slept."

In 1763, the year she committed her heinous crime, La Corriveau was promptly charged with *petit treason*. She was executed on April 10 of that year in a gruesome manner.

According to the closing paragraphs of Kirby's book, Corriveau was "gibbeted" (an archaic term for being hanged) inside an iron cage. Even after she had died, humiliation awaited her: the cage, with her rotting corpse still inside, was left on display for passersby to gawk at.

The indignity to her body seemed to make La Corriveau's spirit restless. The murderous witch's ghost, still encased in the iron cage, was reported to chase people who paused to stare at her mortal remains. Eventually, officials of the church heard about the terrifying apparition that had pursued and frightened calm, credible parishioners. Arrangements were made to perform an exorcism. The first ritual was apparently unsuccessful. A second and then a third attempt at the rite were performed, but according to William Kirby, the manifestation "dragging her cage at her heels" persisted, "defying all the exorcism of the Church to lay her evil spirit to rest."

Those horrid ghostly sightings, and even the phantom's pursuit of terrified mortals, went on undiminished long after La Corriveau's caged decomposed body had been taken down and buried, still in the cage. Some sixty years later, a farmer digging in a field had the misfortune of discovering what Kirby described as the "horrid cage, rusted and decayed." In a rather bizarre twist, the death trap, presumed to be La Corriveau's, was recovered. It was sent to an American museum. As no further documentation exists to prove that the ghost of Marie-Josephte La Corriveau still haunts Quebec City, perhaps a museum in the United States hosts her evil spirit.

Author Val Cleary recounts the story with additional drama in his book *Ghost Stories of Canada*. Because that anthology, published in 1985, is generally catalogued as fiction, it's probable that Mr. Cleary merely wanted to be entertaining, not misleading. Even so, in the interests of presenting as many aspects of this legendary Canadian ghost story as possible, the following twist on the tale is offered.

After interviewing Romeo Dionne, apparently one of La Corriveau's descendants, Cleary wrote that the deceased's caged body remained on display "for more than fifty years." According to this colourful version of the tale, La Corriveau's relatives eventually claimed the cage, and then sought to profit from her crime and suffering. Dionne claimed that the cage still existed, that he knew where it was, and that the ancient rusting mesh was possessed by La Corriveau's angry spirit. His proof? The evil device had been indirectly responsible for at least two deaths.

The first death occurred in 1879, when the cage was on display in an exhibition hall. It was suspended from the ceiling and began to swing about wildly during a windstorm. A metal edge of the contraption hit a kerosene lamp, which started a fire. The flames engulfed the area so quickly that a man nearby was killed in his sleep.

The next victim of the ghastly ghostly murdering spirit, Cleary suggested, was Dionne's own grandfather, who was found in a storage area on his property. His nearly lifeless body was pinned under a fallen pile of scrap metal, which had been stacked very precariously. Resting on the very top was the evil rusted cage. The old man died less than an hour later.

Considering that this ghost story originated in the 1760s and was not recorded in written form until the late 1870s, it isn't surprising that the tale has developed variations. What is both surprising and interesting is that this ghostly piece of Canadiana haunts us into the twenty-first century.

Stage Fright

It seems that in every Canadian province and territory you can see a movie or watch a performance in a haunted theatre. Quebec is certainly no exception. Montreal's Centaur Theatre and its ghosts are happily housed together in a gorgeous old building.

The stately old structure is located on one of Montreal's original cobblestone streets. It dates back to the early 1900s, when it opened as the home of the Montreal Stock Exchange. With its white stone façade and six massive stone pillars, the building revealed that George Post, the American architect who designed it, intended to reflect how important economics were in Canada's burgeoning society. And the building did exactly that for the next sixty-plus years, after which the stock exchange moved to more modern accommodation. Four years later, the Centaur Theatre group breathed entirely new life into the structure by converting it into a world-class theatre.

If those first stockbrokers could see their old offices today, they would hardly recognize the place. The building houses two theatres, an art gallery, and a lounge as well as all the necessary production and administration spaces. One aspect of the property, however, has remained the same, and that's the ghost that haunts the place.

Few people would argue that the grand old building is haunted, but there are two schools of thought on who the resident ghost might be. The most popular notion is that the entity is the spirit of a former stockbroker. Some say they've actually seen the man's ghost, while others just hear him straightening endless sheets of paper—as if he is perpetually trying to keep his work organized. Perhaps he was never able to completely succeed at that chore in life; one version of the phantom stockbroker's story indicates that one stock exchange employee killed himself, and that is why his soul has never left the building.

Other people are sure the haunting is connected with the massive vaults in the basement of the building.

Long-time house manager Layne Shutt had heard all the ghost stories, but he remained a skeptic for years. Then after a particularly long day at work, Shutt went downstairs to complete his routine by making sure that all the areas in the basement were secure. He explained, "I usually start at one end and work my way down the hall. The actors rarely close their doors, and for fire regulations, we have to make sure all the doors are shut."

That night something permanently changed Shutt's perspective on the building he works in. "I started at the north end and locked all the doors. I finally got to the south end and locked the workshop door." By then he was more than ready to leave for home, but as he turned back to take one last look at the doors, he found that "Every single door was wide open."

The man knew for a fact that he was alone in the building. He also knew he had successfully locked each door along that corridor, and he hadn't heard any of the doors open, but, undeniably, there it was: a hallway of wide-open doors. Not knowing what else he could do, he quickly relocked the doors and left the building.

That ghostly prank not only made Layne Shutt a believer, it also made him think that the ghost wasn't a depressed and discouraged middle-aged stockbroker but, rather, a child. It didn't take much investigation to discover that, in the old days of the stock exchange, there would've been many boys in and out of the building on a regular basis. Those children were employed as runners, relaying messages and telegraphs throughout the building and across the street to the telegraph office and back.

A piece of lore that supports that theory tells of a boy who was delivering a message to a broker waiting on the building's balcony. Apparently, in his haste, the boy tripped and fell to the floor below, dying instantly.

Shutt attests, "The things that happen here are not evil or dark. They're more like pranks of a trickster, the things a kid would do, not a fifty-year-old stockbroker."

There is at least one set designer who would agree with that assessment. As the designer tried to get to work painting the stage, the buckets of paint kept tipping over and spilling. The frustrated employee would set the can upright, clean up the spill, and start again—only to find the can on its side just moments later. His co-workers were sympathetic because virtually everyone associated with the Centaur Theatre has seen sourceless shadows flit about and heard music throughout the building when none is being played.

Given the age and the history of the building, it wouldn't be a surprise if more than one ghost is haunting the place. Happily whoever he or they might be, everyone seems content to let them live their afterlife in the magnificent old place.

Anniversary Sightings

On the warm summer's evening of June 27, 1991, an interesting assortment of people was milling about the edges of an abandoned lot at Murray and William streets in the neighbourhood of Griffintown in Montreal, Quebec. Some of those who had gathered were elderly, devout, and filled with nostalgia. Others were younger and barely able to contain their enthusiasm about what might happen next. No one in either group seemed in a hurry to leave. Most had just attended a special mass presided over by one of Griffintown's own, the much-loved Father Thomas McEntee. The priest was born and raised in the close-knit working-class community. The neighbourhood was comprised of decrepit old row houses, and neither the houses nor the people who lived in them ever got the attention they needed. Even so, Father Thomas accomplished a great deal in his life.

During World War II, McEntee served with distinction in the Royal Canadian Navy. All who knew him held him in great esteem as a priest, and in 1990 Father McEntee was awarded the Order of Canada. The man never forgot his humble roots.

And so it was that on the evening of June 27, 1991, the ageing priest said a special mass in his old neighbourhood. He did so again on that same date in 1998 and 2005. He knew those services were important because they gave former neighbours a chance to reunite for a few hours while also commemorating the restless spirit who is said to haunt the area for one night, every seven years.

Like everyone who had grown up in "the Griff," McEntee knew the legend of Mary Gallagher. Parents regularly used her story to frighten their children into obedience. After all, the possibility of encountering an angry headless ghost wandering the streets would encourage all but the most foolhardy youngster to be safely at home before nightfall.

Poor Mary Gallagher's life ended, and her afterlife began, on a warm summer's night just after midnight on June 27, 1879. Mary was thirty-eight years old at the time. She and her younger friend Susan Kennedy had been partying together for several days. Both Mary and Susan liked to carouse, and they weren't overly fussy about their choice of companions. On that particular night, a handsome young stevedore named Michael Flanagan accompanied them.

Around midnight the three made their way to Susan's second-floor digs at 242 William Street, where their good times took a serious turn for the worse as the two women competed for Flanagan's affections. Mary won the competition, but her prize wasn't worth much because by that time he lay passed out on the floor. There were no witnesses to any of this, but clearly Susan was not a gracious loser because, moments later, Mary Gallagher's body also lay on the floor, with her head some distance away.

Michael Flanagan and Susan Kennedy were both charged with Gallagher's murder. Susan was convicted and sentenced to hang on December 5, 1879. Sir John A. Macdonald, Canada's first prime minister, commuted her death sentence to jail time. Flanagan was acquitted entirely due to lack of evidence, but he might as well have been sentenced to death because, by eerie coincidence, his body was found in the Lachine Canal on the very day that Susan was to have been hanged. For months, the grisly murder, the trial, and Flanagan's drowning were the talk of Griffintown, but eventually the wags lost interest and went on to other topics of conversation.

Most accounts indicate that the spirit of Mary Gallagher must have rested peacefully for a number of years, but then in 1900, twenty-one years after her death, there were sightings of her ghost in the rough-and-tumble neighbourhood. In the early 1920s, when interest in spiritualism, ghosts, and communicating with the dead soared, people became even more intrigued with Mary's story, both her life and her afterlife. Folks soon determined that her spirit would appear every seven years, usually on June 27, the anniversary of her death.

There is no denying that the dark narrow streets of Griffintown are the perfect setting for a ghost story, and on October 27, 1928, an article appeared in the *Montreal Star* describing "a bona-fide headless ghost" wandering the streets of Griffintown that was seen "by half a dozen different people in as many nights." The apparition was not just seen but also heard uttering "low and awesome moans." One witness was so terrified by the phantom that he took his bed for days.

The following year, almost to the day, the New York Stock Market crashed heralding the Great Depression. Frivolous talk of ghosts gave way to desperation. Then, in 1939, World War II brought even more horrors into people's lives. Once the war was finally over, people just wanted to get on with their lives. A new era had dawned. Progress was king; the rows and rows of little brick houses that had lined Griffintown's streets were demolished in favour of light industry and parking lots. Finally, in 1970, the remaining heart was ripped out of the old residential area when St. Ann's Church, which had served the community for more than a hundred years, was torn down.

By 1991, Father Thomas McEntee had read an article about the ghost of Mary Gallagher in the *Montreal Gazette* and decided to commemorate the poor restless soul while inviting former neighbours from Griffintown to gather together as they had once done regularly. After the church service, many stayed to visit with one another while others sought a chance to spot Mary Gallagher. No sightings were reported that year, but after Father McEntee's mass in 1998, one woman lingered outside near the spot on William Street where the murder had taken place. The woman called out Mary's name and asked if the murdered soul was present. Moments later, the air grew cold and began to shimmer. The woman called out again. As she did, an image of the old red-brick tenement appeared, and a voice shouted at the witness to "get away from here now!" It doesn't take much imagination to presume that the visitor followed those ethereal instructions.

At this writing, the corner of William and Murray streets is nothing more than an empty lot, but the land won't be barren for much longer. The former slum has been revitalized and is now home to expensive, and much sought after, high-rise housing. A small park, complete with a few ruins, gives a nod to Griffintown's history.

We'll likely never know if residents of any of the new buildings notice a shimmering cold spot in their home. If so, they may be sharing their posh new place with Mary Gallagher's ghost.

By now the tradition of waiting for the long-dead woman's apparition to appear has become so deeply ingrained in the city's culture that June 27 is known as Mary Gallagher Day. This is the power of a ghost story.

For those who are interested in a possible sighting of Mary Gallagher, just make plans to be in Griffintown at the corner William and Murray streets on June 27, 2019. If you miss that day, just mark your calendar for the same date in 2026. Even if Mary's ghost doesn't appear, you're sure to have a unique evening with like-minded people.

Mary Gallagher's ghost is not the only one in Canada said to be seen on the anniversary of her death. On July 8, the apparition of Canadian landscape artist Tom Thomson has been seen paddling his distinctive green canoe on Canoe Lake in Ontario's Algonquin Park. He died under suspicious circumstances on that date in 1917. His body was found in the lake not far from his canoe [see page 109 for full story].

And in Holland Cove, Prince Edward Island, the ghost of a woman is said to emerge from the water on July 14. Her image is so clear that everyone who sees her agrees that she has long black hair and is wearing a full-length white gown. She's seen clearly walking out of the water toward the beach—but only on July 14.

Holy Ghosts

There's no getting around it: The Cathedral of the Holy Trinity in Quebec City, Quebec, has been home to a very active haunting for a very long time. The beautiful old building on Rue des Jardins was completed in 1804, making Holy Trinity the first Anglican cathedral outside the United Kingdom.

Interestingly, the cathedral has likely been haunted from its earliest days. Over the years, its ghost has made herself known to a variety of people, possibly including Queen Elizabeth II. During a royal visit to the church in April 1964, the queen looked up to the second-floor balcony as onlookers watched. It was clear that something up there had caught Her Majesty's attention—and then held it for several minutes. Those who knew the building best didn't wonder what could have caught the royal eye. They knew that spot was one of the ghost's favourite haunts.

Over the years, many people have seen the "shadowy figure of a woman" floating effortlessly between pillars on the second floor. One reliable witness, an organist, stood in bewildered fascination as he heard footsteps approaching him. A few minutes later, the image of a woman dressed in old-fashioned clothing stood before him. The man barely had time to react when the sound of organ music began echoing through the grand space. He beat a hasty retreat, not surprisingly, deciding to postpone his practice session for another day.

Perhaps because organists generally practice when the cathedral empty, they have experienced many of the encounters with the building's spirit. One organist recalled that the ghostly visits usually began with the sounds of interior doors banging closed. As far as he knew he was alone in the church, which made the mysterious noises understandably unnerving. Every time he heard a strange noise he would get up from the organ bench and walk through the building to confirm that he was, indeed, alone.

After making one of those precautionary checks, the man sat back down and organized his sheet music, looking forward to a beneficial practice session. As he did, he could feel a shawl of cold air wrap around his shoulders. The man tried to talk himself out of the sensation, but when he heard loud footfalls moving toward him, he knew he'd had enough for one day. As he picked up his sheet music, movement in his peripheral vision made him look up. He remembers briefly seeing "what appeared to be the shadowy form of a woman." After that he fled from the building.

Another organist was so sure there was a presence nearby that he spoke out loud to it saying, "I know you're here!" With that his sheet music flew from the wind-proof stand and scattered across the floor.

A third musician, whose career involved playing organs at different venues, was in the habit of bringing his calm, well-trained dog with him while he practiced. The animal was used to lying quietly beside his master for hours at a time, even in unfamiliar buildings. But not in the Cathedral of the Holy Trinity. The dog would not settle. Clearly upset, the animal frantically ran through the church and around the pews trying to bite at something his owner could not see. The man was shocked by the dog's behaviour and later explained that the animal had "never bitten or showed any sign of aggression to anyone in his life." That day though, something certainly had the dog agitated and so ended another organist's practice session.

Two very different legends attempt to explain the haunting. The first implicates the deadly cholera epidemic that decimated Quebec in the 1830s. It seems a woman named Iris Dillon, who lived near Rue des Jardins at that time, suffered from narcolepsy and would unexpectedly fall into a deep sleep. Iris worried that while she was suffering from one of these episodes, someone might think that she had died of cholera and carry her sleeping body off for burial. Some say the woman's worst fears came true and that her tortured soul still haunts the church.

Another version of the cause of the haunting was confirmed when a psychic visited the cathedral. The man intuited that, in the late 1800s, a woman killed her own baby and buried the tiny body under some loose floorboards near the cathedral's organ. The ghost, the man discerned, was the infant's mother grieving for her child.

Interestingly, there is a small patch of unmarked concrete in the church floor beside a bishop's crypt that fits with this description.

Could this be the infant's grave? No one knows for certain, but that possibility certainly exists.

Like many cities, Quebec City hosts ghost tours. The tour guides are dressed in long black coats and carry a lantern lit by a candle. The cathedral is an extremely popular stop on the walks—popular with the living, that is, perhaps not so much with the spirit who haunts it.

When tours arrive at the church, the groups are shown in. Then the guide locks the exterior door and begins to talk about the haunting. One evening, the tour was going along as it should; the tourists were all inside and the door was closed and locked. As was her habit, the guide set her lantern on a nearby table. After a moment the candle in the lantern seemed to go out, but the guide didn't let that interrupt her, instead she finished her spiel, knowing she had matches in her pocket and could relight the candle before they left the building.

A few moments later, the feeling of icy tentacles creeping up the guide's legs distracted her. Still, she struggled on. It wasn't until a member of the group complained of chills around her ankles and lower legs that the guide decided the group had been in the cathedral long enough. She pulled the matches out of her pocket and picked up her lantern, but the candle had not just been extinguished, it was gone. No one had been near the marble table where the guide had set the lantern.

That was nearly too much for the guide, but she would have kept her composure and carried on if one of the tourists hadn't approached her as they were heading back outside to say that he'd been distracted by a shadowy figure undulating near the marble table where she'd placed her lantern.

The guide later confessed that the ghost doesn't seem to like the tours, or anyone else for that matter, interrupting her centuries-long haunting, which, of course, makes the cathedral one of the best stops on the tour!

Life-Saving House

Gilles and Marie Bouchard (pseudonyms have been used at the family's request) have often wondered if the house they bought in Quebec's Eastern Townships was haunted or, even more bizarre, somehow imbued with a personality—a protective personality.

The year was 1969, and the property just north of the Vermont border, about 200 kilometres east of Montreal, was going to be a project. That much they knew. There were certainly no modern conveniences in the old, dilapidated farmhouse. The heating consisted of an oil burner in the living room and a wood stove in the kitchen. The bathroom was located a considerable distance from the house.

When the Bouchards began work on the old place, they lived in Montreal during the week and travelled out to their rural property on the weekends with their newborn daughter in tow. Needless to say, the renovation process was slow, but on they worked, even into the cold Quebec winter.

One day in December, they had the oil burner turned up as far as it would go and the wood stove filled with logs, but even so the house was getting colder and colder. When the water pipes froze, they knew the situation was getting serious—especially for their daughter who was asleep nearby. Desperate, they checked both the oil burner and the wood stove. Neither device was even warm to the touch. No wonder the temperature was dropping in the house. They knew they had to stop the work they were doing and head back to the city.

When Marie lifted the baby out of her crib to carry her to the car, the young mother was shocked to find the little girl had a high fever. The worried parents packed up hurriedly and headed for the car. They were just about to lock the front door of the house when both the woodstove and the oil burner began pumping out heat, as they should've been doing all morning.

Within moments the heat was so intense that they had to dampen down both appliances. As a final thought, Gilles turned on the kitchen faucet and was surprised to find that the water was running freely.

They were relieved, but their priority was to get medical help for their child. Gilles drove as quickly as he could with the winter road conditions. Soon they arrived safely at a clinic where the little girl was successfully treated.

To this day, Gilles and Marie are convinced that some force in the old farmhouse caused the heating sources to malfunction in order to draw their attention to their daughter's dangerous condition.

The Bouchards kept the rural property and eventually developed a hobby farm with an assortment of animals. Gilles came to believe that a mischievous ghost haunted the old barn on the premises. He used one plastic scoop in all the different barrels of feed, but no matter where he left that scoop it was missing the next morning. He would always find it but in the most unlikely places, such as on the tractor seat or on the floor, or on a windowsill or up in the hayloft. One day he even found a bale of hay in each of the feed barrels. These hijinks continued all year round even in the winter when there would've been human footprints in the snow around the barn—if the trickster had been human, that is.

It's not too unusual for ethereal beings to play tricks on us corporeal souls, and this seems to have been the case on the Bouchards' farm, but they live with the small annoyances, knowing that the presence may have saved their daughter's life those many years ago.

Frontenac Returns, Briefly

The stately Château Frontenac in Quebec City, Quebec, stands atop Cape Diamond, high above the St. Lawrence River. The hotel is named in honour of Count Frontenac, the explorer who governed New France for nearly twenty years in the 1600s.

The enormous hotel has been a Canadian landmark since it opened its doors on December 20, 1893, offering one hundred and seventy rooms, including three magnificent suites and ninety-three rooms with fireplaces and even bathrooms!

Today the Château Frontenac is even larger, absolutely state-of-the-art, and a designated UNESCO World Heritage Site.

In honour of its one-hundredth anniversary, the hotel underwent a massive renovation in 1993. Interestingly, some of the staff, as well as a few construction workers, felt the presence of long-dead Count Frontenac during the reconstruction process. Nancy Murray, a member of the inn's administrative team, acknowledged that "there were rumours that the place was haunted by Frontenac. He was a very benign spirit who was active only during that time." It was assumed that his spirit had come back to oversee the renovations. After the work was finished, his presence vanished. Today, as far as can be discerned, the Château Frontenac is not haunted.

Murdered Manifestation

Tadoussac, Quebec, is on the north shore of the St. Lawrence River where it meets the Saguenay River. Time's passage has allowed today's residents, for the most part, to remember only the pleasant aspects of their community's past, but at least one citizen is reminded daily that the "good old days" were sometimes brutal and unjust. A man we'll call Pierre understands this fact all too well because he lives in a haunted house.

Although he's fond of his home, he knows it's not entirely his and that experiencing certain unpleasant sensations are part of the price he pays for living there. The room directly above the kitchen is home to the spirit of a maid who worked in the house in the early 1900s. For reasons sadly long forgotten, her employer murdered her. Apparently her soul has never left the room; the maid's presence is still easily detectable her former room, where, it is guessed, the murder took place.

Many people other than the current homeowner have reported being visited by the wronged entity. When she manifests to the living, it is as a feeling that they are not alone, which shouldn't be too surprising because, of course, they are not alone, the ethereal entity is there too.

One guest who was invited to tour the home said, "Cold chills ran through me. I had to leave the room. I was definitely not welcome there."

We can only hope that the poor young soul will finally go to her eternal rest and that the homeowner's companions will only be the flesh-and-blood variety.

Ghostly Footsteps

Lawrence Gilbert and his family moved to an old farmhouse in a rural Quebec in order to run a bar that he and his partners had bought in an old building next door.

One evening, Lawrence and his wife, Eve, were at the bar cleaning up when they both heard someone walking along the upstairs hallway. They presumed they were alone in the building, so Lawrence called his large dog to his side, and together they went upstairs to confront the intruder. They had climbed one short flight of stairs before the dog stopped in his tracks, the fur on the back of his neck standing on end. The dog growled menacingly at first, but then he yelped in fear and ran back down the stairs, leaving his master to continue on his own. The man found the hallway and all the rooms upstairs empty. Only slightly reassured, he went back downstairs.

The couple put the strange occurrence out of their minds until Eve's mother and sister arrived for a Christmas visit. The first night, the two women stayed in rooms on the second floor of the bar. They did not have a restful night. They were kept awake by the sounds of footsteps pacing up and down the hallway.

The next morning, they told Lawrence that he should have told them there was someone else staying in the building. When he confirmed that they had been the only ones in the building, the women moved into the farmhouse with Lawrence and Eve for the rest of the visit.

By then the couple had come to the conclusion that they had a ghost on the second floor of the bar, but they didn't know for certain until the former owner dropped in to see the old place. Over a cup of coffee the man asked, "Does the ghost still haunt the place? The one who walks up and down the hall at night?"

Lawrence was taken aback, but at least he knew that the entity haunting his business investment meant him no harm and probably wasn't even aware of the living beings who shared the space with him. And, really, having spirits at the bar was quite appropriate.

Woman in White

Poor soul, they say that you can hear her pitiful cries long before you see her. The Woman in White has been a fixture of Quebec lore for centuries, and she's still seen and heard today near the Montmorency Falls on the Ile d'Orleans, not far from Quebec City.

The details of the ghostly legend have endured for more than two hundred and fifty years. It seems that Louis Tressier and Mathilde Robin were madly in love and anxious to get married. Mathilde had even been sewing the beautiful white gown that she would wear on their wedding day. Every evening the young couple would meet at the top of Montmorency Falls and happily plan their future, while doing their best to ignore the political strife between the English and the French that swirled around them.

All of that changed on July 31, 1759, when word spread that the English were about to attack French holdings in the New World. Louis bravely joined the resistance, and Mathilde hid with the other women and children, both of them anxious for the battle to be over so that they could get on with their lives.

But Louis was not among the men who returned home. No one knew what happened to him, or even where his body lay. Unable to accept that he had not survived, Mathilde put on the beautiful wedding gown she had painstakingly sewn and set out to search for her beloved.

Near the top of the falls, she was sure she could hear him calling her name. As if she was trying to fly, the young woman spread her arms and leaped off the rocky ledge. Neither Louis nor Mathilde's bodies were ever found, but even today it's said that her mournful wails can be heard over the roar of the falls. Occasionally her image can be seen in the falling water. Locals know not to approach her because it's said that tragedy will befall anyone who touches her beautiful white gown.

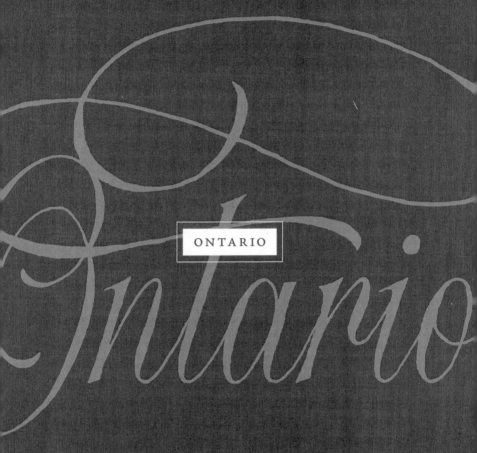

ONTARIO

The Ghosts of Fort George

Fort George at Niagara-on-the-Lake, Ontario, is a fascinating place to tour. Construction of the fort dates back to 1796, but through the magic of creativity, determination, and hard work, you can visit a reconstruction of the fort today. When you're there, you'll get to hear and see scenes from Canada's dramatic past played out by interpreters in period costumes.

Kyle Upton began working at the fort in the early 1990s. He soon developed a fondness for the park, and he's worked there ever since. In the earliest days of his tenure, Kyle heard rumours that the fort was haunted; but his background is in science, so he just scoffed at the tales and wondered who would be naïve enough to believe such nonsense. Nevertheless, it did occur to the young man that creating a special tour based on these ghost stories would offer an alternative way to share his passion for the historic site. And that is how the ghost tours at Fort George were born. It is also how Kyle went from being a skeptic to being a committed believer. He's even written two books about his very haunted workplace, *Niagara's Ghosts* (1999) and *Niagara's Ghosts at Fort George* (2004).

As for the ghost tours themselves, they've become more and more popular each year. They've also become more detailed and even scarier because tourists who have paranormal encounters as they're being guided through the old site often share those experiences with the group's leader.

This was certainly the case with a building known as Blockhouse I. Kyle remembers that when he began hosting the tours in 1994, he didn't know of any ghost stories from that structure. It didn't take long, though, to hear some surprising comments from visitors. People would often tell him that they saw a shadowy figure standing at a window and that the image seemed to be watching as the group passed by. Other folks were sure they had seen a figure pacing back and forth behind that same window.

Despite those sightings, Kyle had never seen that particular ghost himself, and so he presumed that whatever it was that people were reacting to could be explained rationally. After all, he knew that the fort's evening light could play tricks on people's eyes and make a person see what really isn't there. Two years later, Kyle had a change of heart. He remembers that it was close to midnight and he was alone, securing the fort for the night.

"The depths of darkness had settled about the rampart. This is when the atmosphere of the fort changes," he explains. "The air thickens to the point of oppressiveness and a haze settles into the corners of your vision, only to vanish as you turn to confront it. One night as I sped to escape from what had become a less-than-comfortable Fort George, I looked up into the lit window of Blockhouse I to find its light occluded by the shadowy form that filled the aperture."

He'd certainly encountered spirits in the fort, but he recalls, "This one hit me at a purely emotional level. I was filled with such a gut-level feeling of terror that I contemplated climbing over the ten-foot-high palisades to escape from the fort rather than risk walking past that building to the front gate." Instead he took cover in the brightly lit staff building until he'd calmed his nerves. When he went out again, the manifestation was gone, and the fort felt normal again. Even so, to this day he "takes pains not to look into that window after the sun has set."

He no longer wonders why some people were so upset when they looked at the window of Blockhouse I.

Another wraith who haunts the property is the spirit of a girl. She is certainly not a threatening figure. It's believed that her name is some variation of Sarah Anne. This little wraith joined the tours in 1999 and is frequently seen standing just outside the tunnel where the guided ghost walks begin. Kyle believes that the child's presence doesn't go into the tunnel because that structure didn't exist when she was alive.

When a psychic visited the fort, she was quick to identify the little girl's presence and said that the child's name was Sarahann. Next, a genealogist became curious about the small figure and approached the puzzle from a different perspective. After checking historical documents and searching gravestones in the nearby cemetery, a genealogy researcher concluded that the ghost was called Sarah Anne in life and that she died as a child in 1740.

"That's not a story we tell on the tours though," Kyle acknowledges. Even so, it's not at all uncommon to see the little girl's apparition standing at the opening of the tunnel.

Families are always welcome at the fort, so there are frequently youngsters along on the tours. As the tourists assemble, families sometimes hang back a bit from the rest of the group to make sure that their children won't feel frightened in the crowded tunnel. One evening, a mother with two girls, ages seven and nine, waited while thirty or so people sorted themselves into a clutch in the dark, confining tunnel. Unfortunately, this put them farthest away from the only source of light: the leader's lantern.

Thinking that her daughters might need some reassurance in the dark and unfamiliar place, the mother reached down and clasped one small hand in hers before reaching her other hand slightly behind her body to take the other child's hand. Assured that her children were both all right, the woman began to listen to their leader's introduction. Soon it was time to follow the tour guide to the next location. As the crowd started to move, the woman heard a child's voice cry out from the middle of the group. "Mommy, Mommy, where are you?" It was her older daughter's voice. Seconds later the family was reunited, but the experience left the woman puzzled.

"I thought you were right beside me," she said to the nine-year-old who confessed that she'd left her mother's side as soon as the leader began talking. The child had assumed that her mother and younger sister had followed her into the crowd. But of course they hadn't. The mother had stayed back by the entrance linking hands with her seven-year-old and, she thought, her older daughter. But if the nine-year-old had been standing by the tour guide the whole time, then whose small hand had rested so comfortably in her other palm? The answer to that question has never been confirmed, but Kyle and others presume that the Fort's little girl just wanted some physical human contact.

Kyle's friend William Foster came to work at Fort George one summer. The man was a physics major and extremely skeptical about anything to do with the supernatural. When he initially heard that there were ghost tours at Fort George, he assumed actors dressed up in old clothing and scared the tourists. When he learned that this was not the case, he was incredulous that his co-workers were naïve enough to believe in ghosts. On his last night at the fort, though, William joined a ghost tour, more to say goodbye to the friends he'd made over the summer and to pay his respects to the fort.

William stepped away from the group, intending to take a moment alone to appreciate the place that he had come to love. He was about to catch up to the rest of the group when he heard a footstep on the gravel beside him. He looked toward the noise, but night had fallen and his eyes couldn't pierce the gloom. He called out asking who was there. His only reply was the sound of footsteps moving closer to him.

William called out to the group's guide, but no one heard him. Then there was another footstep on the gravel, even closer this time. Something was coming for him. He couldn't see it, but he could certainly feel it. The young physicist tried to run, but he was so frightened that his legs were uncoordinated, and he tumbled backward, screaming. The group tour heard the commotion and ran to see if

William was all right. They found the man huddled on the ground. Just as they arrived to offer help, he sensed the presence retreat.

William eventually recovered from his experience and, aside from that event, still holds fond memories of his time at Fort George. He did, however, warn Kyle to be careful because "There are some things in Fort George that don't like us in their fort." Kyle has never forgotten his friend's admonition.

Not all the ghost stories from Fort George are quite that frightening, however. A phantom named Irving, for instance, is a most benign presence. He's seen in the upper floor of the soldiers' barracks building, so presumably he was a soldier. He can make a nuisance of himself sometimes, with odd noises and moving things about, but mostly he seems happy just to be seen and acknowledged.

Another ghostly presence at the fort is one they call the Watcher. "Seeing that one is rarer these days than it used to be. Perhaps his energy is starting to dissipate," Kyle speculates.

Another phantom at the fort is "the man in white." He lies on beds in the soldiers' quarters, content to merely watch the tourists go by. And sometimes photographs catch unexplained images, even though picture-takers didn't see anything unusual. The apparition of a stern-looking woman has been seen but only as a reflection in one particular mirror. In addition, sourceless shadows are seen and disembodied voices heard. Doors open and close when no one is near them—all classic signs of a haunting.

Is it any wonder that Canada Post chose Fort George as one of the haunted places to feature on a postage stamp? Do visit, if you dare.

The Haunted Hockey Hall of Fame

Sadly, in order to have a ghost story, there must first be a death. Some ghost stories are so old that the identity of the person has been lost in the mists of time, but even when that is the case, it's important to respect the fact that the person once had a place on this earth and grieving loved ones.

The Bank of Montreal at Yonge and Front streets in downtown Toronto, Ontario, was built in 1885. Canada's economy was booming, and the bank building reflected that prosperity. Its main hall was a soaring two-storey structure topped with a decorative dome and surrounded by a mezzanine with a spectacular view. This was a building that intended to impress—and it did. Over the course of nearly a hundred years, millions of dollars exchanged hands within these grand walls, but by the early 1980s, the branch was badly outdated and closed its doors for the last time. In the early 1990s, the splendid old place found a worthy new purpose; it is now home to Canada's Hockey Hall of Fame.

The historic building has been incorporated into a modern downtown high-rise office complex and the juxtaposition of the old architecture with the new is dramatic. The arrangement has also served to preserve the bank's ghost, Dorothy.

In the early 1950s, Dorothy worked in the bank as a teller. By all reports she was a pretty nineteen-year-old who was a popular staff member because she was always smiling and cheerful. Some say she was involved in a one-sided love affair, and this may be so. Whatever the circumstances were, they were clearly too much for Dorothy to bear.

On the morning of March 11, 1953, Dorothy arrived at the bank earlier than expected. Len Redwood, chief messenger for the bank at the time, had already started work for the day. At first he was pleasantly surprised to see Dorothy because she was considered one of the nicest people on staff. Redwood was quoted some years after the incident as saying she was "always smiling."

The man's surprise turned to concern when he realized the young woman looked "pretty rough," as though she'd had a tough night. He noted that Dorothy went straight into the second-floor women's washroom. After a considerable length of time, the young woman emerged from the toilet facilities, went downstairs for a moment, and then returned to the washroom. Seconds later, a shot rang out. Dorothy lay dead on the washroom floor. She had killed herself with a single shot to the head, using the standard bank-issue revolver. (In those days, banks kept firearms available for the staff. In the case of a robbery, workers were expected to defend their employer's funds by shooting at anyone who tried to rob them.)

Signs of the haunting began almost immediately. Dorothy's female co-workers refused to use the upstairs washroom where the woman had died. They all reported feeling distinctly uncomfortable in the room. Eventually the Bank of Montreal gave in and built new toilet facilities in the basement.

That expense did not provide complete protection from Dorothy's presence. Staff said they could feel her everywhere. Lights went on and off by themselves. Doors that had been securely locked were found open, and some people felt a hand pressing their shoulder or leg. Everyone agreed that it was the pitiful wailing, the screams and moans, that was the most difficult to accept.

When he was interviewed in the 1980s, retired bank clerk Len Redwood recalled that members of the staff often reported that they felt as though they were being watched even though no one was looking at them. Well, no one alive. In addition, items that employees required in their daily duties would often go missing for a period of time, only to turn up later, just as mysteriously, at an unexpected place.

The custodial staff was perhaps the most severely affected. As they worked away in the dark and quiet of night, they frequently reported hearing unexplainable sounds, some as distressing as shrieking and moaning. But the business of commerce had to go on, and the employees accepted the haunting as best they were able. Perhaps when the branch closed they were all relieved to either retire or be transferred to a more mundane workplace.

The once-glorious old Bank of Montreal building remained mostly vacant for the next ten years.

When the Hockey Hall of Fame first took over the premises in 1993, many employees clocked some very late hours in order to complete everything that needed to be done for the official opening. One night, two people who'd been working overtime finally decided to leave for the night, and one employee asked the other what he or she had been doing going up and down the stairs so much.

"What do you mean, what was I doing?" came the reply. "What were you doing? I was at my desk the whole time."

The incorrect assumption that it was their colleague they were hearing wandering around the building had provided both of them with peace of mind while they completed their chores.

Christine Simpson, who was in charge of public relations for the Hall of Fame at the time of its opening, made reference to the ghost story as she escorted a group of people through the facility. One woman in the group apparently looked frantic when she heard this news because she said that she had distinctly felt an invisible presence only moments before.

Children are generally much more likely to see an apparition than adults are; so it was in 1995 when a child was touring the exhibits with his adult family members. Suddenly, for no reason discernable to the adults in the group, the boy stopped in his tracks. One them asked the child what was wrong. The little boy pointed off into what appeared to be empty space. When questioned further he exclaimed over and over, "Can't you see her? Can't you see her?"

When the boy realized that no, in fact, the adults with him could not see what he was seeing, he described the image. He was describing Dorothy.

By now, regardless of whether Dorothy actually continues to move items around in the former bank building, she is occasionally, but good-naturedly, blamed for such mischief if anything goes missing.

Apparently the tragically jilted bank teller lives on amid Canada's tributes to our country's hockey heroes. We wish her well and hope she enjoys the ghosts of Canada's national sport.

Drowned Towns

An abandoned car, an empty swimming pool, an unoccupied building—they're all just a bit creepy. It's no wonder then that ghost towns are unnerving places; all those empty buildings, the roads devoid of traffic, and the stillness where people once lived busy and productive lives. An even creepier sight would be an underwater ghost town. That might sound like something out of a horror movie, but there are six submerged towns lying at the bottom of the St. Lawrence Seaway between Cornwall and Kingston, Ontario.

Back in the 1950s, the Canadian government realized that in order to improve shipping, the St. Lawrence River would have to be widened and deepened. This was a lofty goal. Dams that had protected half a dozen small towns along the river's shore would have to be destroyed and the residents moved to new communities.

Likely due to good planning and execution, the mammoth undertaking went off without a hitch. On July 1, 1958, twenty-five thousand people gathered to watch the last dam exploded, releasing a torrential wave of water. As the flood surged, the water buried the remains of the once-snug towns and all the land around them—including more than five thousand graves.

History proves that the project did have the economic benefit that was intended, but there has also been an unintended benefit. The "drowned towns" have become a haven for SCUBA divers. With air tanks strapped to their backs and flippers on their feet, divers swim in and around the buildings that, for one reason or another, were left on their original sites, cemeteries and all.

The dive sites aren't for the faint of heart. Divers exploring the drowned towns say they often feel as though someone is watching them. Others have seen shapes moving about, and sailors have seen lights shining weakly from below the water's black surface. The scariest encounters though are the disembodied and indistinct voices emanating from the towns that lie in their watery graves. Perhaps a few souls are continuing their day-to-day lives unaware that the waters of the St. Lawrence Seaway have buried their hometowns.

Midway Madness

Amusement parks are always full of fun and, surprisingly often, full of ghosts. Some of the original rides at Disneyland have been replaced, but their haunted folklore remains active. It is said that the ghost of a teenage boy who died on the PeopleMover haunts the ride. Former staff and even some visitors to the park were convinced that the lad's spirit never left the spot where he died. There have also been ghostly rumours about three other displays, including Tom Sawyer's Island where people say they've seen sourceless shadows and undulating shapes.

But of course Disneyland is in the United States. Canadian carnivals aren't haunted, are they? Apparently the answer is yes—Canada does have its share of amusement anomalies.

One of those haunted parks is near Toronto, Ontario. A former employee, who asked to be referred to by his middle name, John, has quite a tale to tell. The ride in question was a roller coaster that, interestingly, has since been dismantled.

John recalls that the well-run amusement park had a strict safety code and that the roller coaster was thoroughly inspected every morning to make sure there were no problems. Early one summer morning, during a routine inspection, there was a freak accident. Details were sketchy, but it seems that the ride began to move while the inspector was climbing on it. Sadly, the man was killed.

Needless to say, the ride was shut down immediately. It was never reopened, but the rails were salvaged and used on a new ride. Right from the start, that replacement ride seemed to have brought an uncomfortable aura about it. Even the booths for nearby games of chance, which had always operated smoothly before, began to start and stop when there was no one near them. John says that the area had become a maintenance nightmare.

At night after the park is closed, bells, whistles, and sirens that seem to be coming from everywhere and nowhere have been known to startle the staff. Some mornings, prizes, such as stuffed animals, turn up in very strange places—certainly not where they were left the night before.

Power sources are frequently implicated in hauntings, and this was the case in one building where power cuts were a regular occurrence. John adds that the door to that building could also "be a challenge." Apparently it was always easy enough to get in, but trying to leave the place was another matter. Sometimes it felt as if someone was pushing against the door trapping you inside.

But of course, John says, the show must go on. "Maintenance crews were constantly fixing the problems: the games, the lights, the door's hinges, even new locks on the door, but nothing helped. As soon as repairs are completed, things break down again. Also, the staff turnover in that area is always high."

Could the ghost of the maintenance worker who was killed on the job be trying to make his presence known as a reminder of the potential danger?

John concludes his chilling tale with these comments: "The park staff was certain there was some sort of supernatural phenomenon alive there. And, as far as I know, it's there still."

Haunted Museum

The Canadian Museum of Nature was designed to look like a gothic castle complete with twisting staircases, gargoyles, and grotesques. Looking at the place, you'd think it was haunted—and you would be right. A veritable laundry list of activity has been reported from the grand old structure on McLeod Street in Ottawa, Ontario.

The building holds thousands of artefacts; each piece has its own natural and, in some cases, supernatural history.

Cleaners working through the night have watched doors mysteriously open when no one is near them—no one visible, that is. Once an enormous undulating "wave of shadow" moved across a dinosaur display, and other shadows occasionally cascade through various corridors and rooms of the museum. No physical source was ever found for these strange, dark forms.

A security guard remembered seeing a partially formed silhouette of a human figure. She described the form as slightly transparent with the head and shoulders being more defined than the body. On the fourth floor, a worker was stunned to see an apparition floating nearby. The corporeal and ethereal beings locked eyes for a moment. Although ghosts rarely seem aware of their current-day surroundings, a certain woman working at the Natural History Museum is sure that the apparition of a young man tried, unsuccessfully, to communicate to her. She was disappointed that the connection between them never became strong enough for an exchange of information.

Occasionally people working in the museum get the uncomfortable feeling that they are being watched even though they know they are alone. When this happened to one woman, she looked around and saw a human-like image reflected in a mirror. Frozen with fear, she watched the misty shape move away from the mirror and across the room before passing through her own, temporarily paralyzed, body. Moments later, the vision vanished.

The museum once hosted a special exhibit about folklore and superstitions. Not surprisingly, the display brought its own supply of supernatural energy. There were displays of a broken mirror, a cracked sidewalk, and a leaning ladder set among trinkets imbued with magical powers—or thought to be. A long-time museum employee, the technical services director at the time, declared that the exhibit brought together "too much hocus-pocus and witchcraft in one place." The next day a stone mask locked in a display case turned itself a hundred and eighty degrees between the time the museum closed that night and opened the next morning.

Both security guards and cleaners report walking through patches of either cold or hot air. These are classic signs of a haunting, as are elevators that go up and down of their own accord and alarms that ring when there's no cause to.

Rumour has it that a medium once visited the haunted museum and tried to exorcise the supernatural occupants. It's not known whether the attempt was entirely successful or not.

Paddling into Eternity

Like the story of Mary Gallagher on page 82, the following legend is an anniversary haunting.

Tom Thomson, one of Canada's most renowned landscape painters, was only thirty-nine years old when he died on July 8, 1917. The circumstances of his death have never been certain, but what is known is that Thomson's body was found floating near the shore of Canoe Lake in Ontario's Algonquin Park. The cause of death was ruled an accidental drowning, but no one who knew the man believed that could have been the case. The artist was a skilled outdoorsman who was well familiar with his surroundings; it was unthinkable that he could simply have fallen out of his canoe and drowned. Many people were convinced that the man had been killed during a party at a friend's cottage.

Worse, the disturbing circumstances continued even after the man's death. Thomson's friends had buried him near the shore of Canoe Lake, but his parents wanted to bring their son home. They asked for the remains to be disinterred and sent to them for reburial. Digging up a body is never a pleasant task, but in this case the chore was also shrouded in mystery, with some believing that another coffin, one weighted down with stones instead of a body, was sent to the Thomson family.

It's not much wonder then that the painter's soul has not rested in peace but has lingered at his beloved Canoe Lake.

It's said that, even now, more than a century on, Tom Thomson's ghost can be seen paddling near the shoreline of Canoe Lake—but only on July 8 of each year. Witnesses report watching in fascination as the image of a man in a canoe appears through the early morning mists, recognizable by his checked shirt and distinctive boat.

The Tom Thomson ghost story has attracted its fair share of skeptics, but over the years reputable citizens have described seeing this anniversary haunting. Some even say they have spoken to the apparition and others claim Thomson's image has given them a cheery wave.

This anniversary haunting has become a Canadian legend as distinctive as Tom Thomson's famous paintings of rugged rural Ontario.

Successful Séances

Canada's longest-serving prime minster, William Lyon Mackenzie King, held that office during three different time periods for a total of more than twenty years. He was a polarizing leader, and even today, historians are divided about whether he was a great leader or a gullible fool. What is known for certain is that King was a devoted spiritualist who spent hundreds of hours in séances, contacting the souls of the dead.

Many of these supernatural sessions took place in King's home with his friend Joan Patteson. The pair created a system to contact an amazing assortment of spirits who were, in their words, "beyond the veil." They both must have been extremely patient people because their method relied on a piece of furniture that King always referred to as "the little table." One of the table's legs would tap on the floor. A single tap indicated the letter "A," two taps was the letter "B," and so on. Their code may have been time consuming but apparently it was successful. They claimed to have summoned the souls of an assortment of historical figures including Leonardo da Vinci, Theodore Roosevelt, famed British leader William Gladstone, and even the ghosts of King's three dogs, all named Pat. One consistent visitant was the presence of the King's mother, Isabel Mackenzie King. The prime minister's devotion to her is a matter of public record. After her death, he created something of a shrine to her memory in his home. He placed a framed photograph of her in a place of honour and always left a lamp lit beside that photo.

Today, King's former home is a public museum with the third-floor study set up as it was during his lifetime. The photograph and the lamp are prominently displayed. To be respectful and historically accurate, the lamp is turned on during the day, but at night it is turned off. Sometimes, though, the lamp comes back on even though no one's been near it.

A security guard remembers switching the light off before he went downstairs, but as his foot landed on the bottom step he heard a light switch click. He went back upstairs to make sure that nothing was wrong and found the lamp beside the photo of Mrs. King burning brightly. He turned the light off again and went downstairs a second time. Once again, as he reached the bottom of the stairs he heard the click. He went back up to the study. When he saw that the lamp was turned on again, he decided not to argue with the ghost of William Lyon Mackenzie King, especially over matters concerning the deceased man's mother.

Security guards aren't the only ones to see that light burning when it should be off. Neighbours have seen a light shining through the upstairs window long after the museum was closed for the night.

Mackenzie King also owned an estate in Quebec's Gatineau Park, across the Ottawa River from the city of Ottawa, Ontario, and his ghostly image has been seen there several times. His spirit seems to be enjoying the beautiful property into eternity.

Whether you admire him or not, you have to give William Lyon Mackenzie King credit for being an enduring Canadian presence.

Talking Statue

The story about an old statue in Burlington, Ontario, may not be a ghost story per se, but it certainly is one of the eeriest tales in Canada.

The bronze art piece bears the likeness of a World War I soldier and stands atop a 3-metre-high granite base. There are many memorials much like this one all across Canada, but none are exactly like the statue in Burlington—this statue is rumoured to move and to speak.

Strange stories have followed the statue through moves from one location in the city to another and finally to its location today, near city hall.

When locals gather in silence to pay their respects on Remembrance Day, people claim to have heard the footfalls of soldiers marching and voices barking orders. There are even those who claim to have seen the solid piece of inanimate bronze move.

Ghost Station

The subway system in Toronto, Ontario, transports millions of passengers over dozens of routes every year. The system is well marked with signs and works efficiently.

That's why it's odd that, in 1966, authorities permanently closed a connecting station just six months after opening it. Two explanations were given. The first was that if there were a breakdown on one line, it would cause delays throughout the system. The second, much less likely, reason was that passengers were getting confused about how to get into and out of the new lower station.

Whatever the reason, the station was abandoned. Since then it has only been used for storage and is occasionally rented out as a backdrop for television and movie productions. Many people who've spent time in the abandoned station swear that it's haunted.

Like the old Chris de Burgh love song, the ghost in the abandoned station is known as the Lady in Red. It seems she is just as unforgettable, but for all the wrong reasons. She floats slowly along in mid-air, her empty eye sockets like bottomless black holes and her red dress flowing behind her. And then, just as slowly, she vanishes from sight.

No one knows who the entity is or why she haunts the abandoned subway station. History buffs, though, are quick to point out that in preparation to excavate for the subway, an old "potter's field," a burial ground for the poor, was dug up, and the corpses were moved to another cemetery. Perhaps the removal disturbed at least one soul who had previously been resting in peace.

Haunted Hostel

Where else but in Ottawa, Ontario, our nation's capital, could you find such funky overnight accommodation? The building is an old, imposing-looking stone structure that completely lacks any of the welcoming feeling most hotels project. And there's a good reason for that. This hotel, or hostel, was built in 1862 as the Carleton Jail.

For a hundred and ten years, the jail held some of the worst specimens of the human race—as both guards and inmates. Over the years, those stone walls have echoed with the screams of many inmates; jail guards are rumoured to have beaten and even killed some prisoners. Immigrants unfortunate enough to have arrived in Ottawa suffering from cholera, scarlet fever, or any other dreadful contagious disease were isolated in the jail's cold, damp basement and left to die. Then their bodies were incinerated and the ashes buried on the grounds.

Not surprisingly, the souls of these anguished wretches have haunted the building ever since. Current-day guests have seen sourceless shadows and heard the pathetic cries of children who died a century ago or more. Hostel guests have been touched and even pushed by invisible hands. The huge cell doors rattle when no one is near them. The sound of men's voices wail from empty rooms.

Despite all of this supernatural activity, or possibly because of it, the hostel regularly attracts young travellers who are looking for low-priced accommodation with spirit, so to speak.

Phantom of the Opera House

The Gordon Lightfoot Auditorium is housed within the elegant old Orillia Opera House in Orillia, Ontario, and a very unusual pianist occasionally offers a recital on the stage there. The musician's repertoire is limited to sad-sounding songs that are only heard when the house is empty. No one knows who the talented musician is because the pianist has never been seen, despite the number of times these tunes have been heard. When employees hear the phantom music, they make their way through the hall to the stage, but by that time the music has stopped and the phantom has vanished. Perhaps he or she is somehow connected to the disembodied sounds of laughter and applause that occasionally echo through the auditorium when it seems to be empty.

Ghostly Organist

In Uptergrove, Ontario, an ethereal entity once gave a brief concert in St. Columbkille's Church. Many years ago, parishioners were busy cleaning the church and preparing for the Easter service. The volunteers were shocked to see a formally dressed man sitting at the keyboard of the church's organ. The image was so clear that the witnesses were able to describe his clothes: an old-fashioned black suit and a top hat. They also noticed that the man's face was unnaturally pale and white.

Two of the women mustered up the courage to confront the man. As they approached, he stood up and walked through a door and out of sight. Thinking that they knew the layout of the church better than their musical visitor, the two followed him through that door. They knew the space was merely an anteroom, with no other door and no windows, so they were sure they had him cornered. They were wrong, though; the tiny space was completely empty. The phantom organist had disappeared.

The Bell Mansion

William and Katherine Bell moved to Sudbury, Ontario, just before the turn of the last century. Within a few years, they were by far the wealthiest couple in the city, and they built themselves a home to reflect that wealth. The Bells were both extremely involved with the community and supported many organizations.

William died in 1945 when he was eighty-seven years old. Katherine stayed on in their enormous home until her death in 1954. The Bells had no descendants and had bequeathed their enormous house to the local hospital. The beautiful old place served as a nurses' residence for a number of years before being gutted by a fire. From then until 1966, Belrock, as the Bells called their palatial estate, stood empty, its interior in ruins and its doors and windows covered with sheets of plywood.

What was to happen to the once-gorgeous old place? With the exception of one small room, the conservatory, the fire had burned away any historical significance in the building's interior. Fortunately, arrangements were made, and the house soon became the home of Sudbury's art gallery.

It didn't take long for the home's new occupants to discover that Katherine Bell had not yet left the building.

Footsteps are heard walking along the second floor when that area is known to be empty. The apparition of a grand-looking woman dressed in clothing from another era has been seen in one of the galleries. The image was so real and solid looking that the witness presumed she was human—until she vanished.

When a security guard was alone in the building and feeling a little uneasy, she began to sing. Much to her shock, an unseen presence in the house seemed to pick up her tune.

Not every art gallery can lay claim to a musical ghost!

MANITOBA

A Very Haunted House

Once upon a time, there was a very old house on Manitoba Avenue in Winnipeg, Manitoba. But the story of this house is no fairy tale. This is the true story of a very haunted home.

The house was more than forty years old when Eva Pip's father bought it in 1953 as a surprise for his wife and daughter. Unfortunately, the purchase wasn't the happy surprise he had hoped it would be. First of all, the house was flat-out ugly, with its unpainted grey bricks and limestone block foundation, but that alone wouldn't have spurred Eva's mother's dramatic reaction. The moment she saw the place she began to sob, saying that it seemed "very unpleasant and depressing."

Nevertheless, the house was theirs, and so the family went inside. While her parents looked around the main floor, Eva, who was only three years old at the time, climbed the staircase. There was a closet right at the top of the stairs. As the girl stood in front of that closet door, she was suddenly paralyzed by an overwhelming fear. She wasn't even able to call out for one of her parents to come and get her. After what seemed like a very long time to the little girl, her mother finally came to rescue her.

Sadly, the horrors both Eva and her mother felt had to be put aside because this was now their home and would be for the next twenty-five years.

Phantom footsteps echoed through the house, especially by the front door. Often the sourceless sounds moved up the staircase, each stair creaking as an invisible presence made its way to the top. The sounds would stop in front of the closet door that had so terrified

Eva. Some days, when she felt brave enough, Eva would look up the stairs and see the door slowly open and close by itself.

This was not a case of a child's overactive imagination because Eva's parents also heard footsteps throughout the house. Every time Eva's father heard the phantom sounds, he scoured the house for intruders but never found anyone—no one visible anyway.

Eva's parents both worked, and so she spent many terrified hours in the house alone as a child. She developed a habit of sitting with her back pressed up against a wall so that nothing could come at her from behind. While that posture made her feel somewhat safer, there were other activities that were virtually guaranteed to cause a supernatural response. When Eva played the piano, for instance, she would often hear "an enormous crash" like wood splintering. The sound always came from the base of the staircase. Every time it happened, the girl would get up from the piano and check, but she never found anything that could've caused the sound.

But this spectre wasn't content just to let himself be felt and heard. He was also frequently seen. Eva recalled the terror of waking up to find the image of a man standing in her room. The apparition was so clear that she could make out his brown hair and knew he was middle-aged. Her mother saw the same figure in broad daylight. Once the phantom squeezed the woman's fingers to get her attention. He looked so real that she was sure the man had somehow broken into the house. She followed him as he moved into the kitchen. Then he dissolved before her eyes.

One phantom sound was only ever heard in Eva's bedroom. She described the noise as sounding as if someone was bouncing a ball. After each bounce there would be "a peculiar scraping noise," she recalled. This pattern of sounds would go on for hours at a time.

This haunting was clearly a full-blown poltergeist intrusion, and in true poltergeist fashion, this wraith liked to play tricks on the living. Eva had an old wind-up-style alarm clock in her bedroom. She would periodically hear the clock's ticking getting quieter and quieter before stopping completely. Then, even though no one had been near it, the clock would start running again.

Random objects around the house would fall off walls and shelves, and the family would find pictures and other decorations on the floor. Other small items would disappear entirely only to reappear later in another part of the house. Once the sliver of a bone manifested at the top of the stairs near the closet door. Eva didn't even want to think about where that might have come from. The incident did, though, help to confirm her suspicions that the nerve centre for whatever unnatural being permeated the house was linked to the closet. When the Pips found that there was a sealed space behind the closet they didn't dare investigate it.

One day, Eva's mother decided to take some pictures of her daughter and asked Eva to pose at the bottom of the staircase. When her mother pressed the shutter release, the flash was unusually bright. When she tried the shot a second time, nothing happened at all. Her mother investigated and found that there were no batteries in the flashgun. How had it flared up the first time? Likely no one will ever know.

Unfortunately, the entity was not at all shy and would often make his presence known when guests were in the house. Eva explained that, over the years, "dozens of other people also witnessed the footsteps, the crashes with no apparent cause, and other phenomena."

The Pip family shared their house with a nasty paranormal presence for more than twenty-three years before selling the place and moving out in 1976. They had finally escaped the terror, but the haunting didn't stop. Soon after the new owners moved in, they found the basement filled with black water. This had never happened when the Pips had lived there, and there hadn't been any recent rainstorms. Perhaps it was the ghost's way of announcing his presence to the new owners.

Then, in 1992, a terrible coincidence occurred in the Pip family's life. First Eva's mother was diagnosed with an incurable cancer. Just a few days later, their former home, the place they'd all struggled to live in for twenty-three years, was ravaged by fire.

Eva Pip has gone on to have a successful life as a scientist, but she's never forgotten the horrors of that house. The experience of growing up there convinced her that there is a dimension that humans do not comprehend. In light of all the events that went on in that nondescript, grey-brick house on Manitoba Avenue, it's difficult to argue that opinion.

Delta Marsh

In the 1930s, a wealthy Winnipeg businessman named Donald Bain had a lodge built near the Delta Marsh, on the south shore of Lake Manitoba, roughly 20 kilometres north of Portage la Prairie, Manitoba. That location was not chosen by coincidence. Bain loved to hunt ducks, and waterfowl were plentiful there, hence he named the place Mallard Lodge. Soon the rich and famous made their way to enjoy Bain's rustic getaway. At least two Hollywood superstars of the day, Cary Grant and Clark Gable, were known to have enjoyed time at the lodge.

In order to keep the lodge running smoothly, Bain hired a full-time caretaker, a man named Murray, who ran the lodge and looked after the specially trained dogs necessary for duck hunting. By all accounts Murray was totally dedicated to his job and made sure that every guest's needs were met. He also tended skillfully to the dogs. In short, Mallard Lodge was Murray's life.

When Donald Bain died in 1962, the lodge on Delta Marsh sat vacant for some years. There was even talk of tearing down the carefully crafted old place. Fortunately in 1966, the University of Manitoba took over the property as an ecological research station with the lodge serving as the administrative headquarters. This situation worked well for everyone until 2011, when the station was permanently closed leaving behind some "spirited" history.

University employee Russ Mead, the research station's long-serving manager, came to know some of that history very well, and it didn't take him long to recognize that he was sharing his workplace with a ghost. Mead's accepting nature must have helped him adapt, but apparently so did the spectre's disposition. "Murray's a friendly ghost," he attested.

Apparently, in the early days of the building's incarnation as a field station, Murray made his presence well known. "He would open and close doors. Turn on faucets and lights or monkey around with the thermostat."

Mead wondered if the fact that the building had been vacant for so long had something to do with the strength of the haunting. He might have been correct because many true ghost stories imply that ghostly activity increases when a building is empty.

One summer, a couple was staying at the lodge alone over the August long weekend—or at least they thought they were by themselves. As it turned out, Murray was also present. He watched them from an upstairs window as they made their way up the driveway, and he also managed to ring a huge cast-iron bell on top of a pole.

That bell figured in another couple's experience. Kelly and Adrian arrived at the lodge in the wee hours of the morning: 2:30 a.m., to be precise. There was no one else at the property that night, and yet as they drove past the pole with the bell on top, the bell started to ring. The two watched in fascinated horror as the bell's clapper moved in a slow controlled way.

As the pair walked toward the lodge, they could see a light shining from a second-floor window and a figure silhouetted in the glass. As they got closer, the window went dark and the image disappeared.

Kelly took a flashlight and searched the building but could not find any trace of anyone having been there. There were no other cars in the parking lot, nor were there any boats at the shore. They concluded that Murray had been watching them as they arrived at the lodge.

Biologists often stayed at the Delta Marsh field station for a number of days at a time. As scientists, their work with the natural world must be as precise as possible. These are not people given to flights of fancy. Despite this, a graduate student named Michael, who was well known for being meticulous, had an experience that could only be explained by the supernatural.

Michael had turned in for the night, but for some reason he hadn't been able to fall asleep. Frustrated, he sat up in bed and reached for the flashlight he had left on the nightstand. But the tabletop was bare. This surprised and annoyed the young man because he knew he had put the light there less than an hour before. Where could it be? He looked around the room—and that is when he saw a skull floating near the end of his bed. He looked again and realized that there wasn't just a skull but an entire body, draped in black. The image then floated over the bed and out of sight.

Michael came away from his fieldwork that year with bragging rights to the scariest ghost story from the station at the Delta Marsh.

There have also been fleeting sightings of phantom dogs in the lodge. People have seen dogs going up a staircase beside the image of a person. Other folks have heard dogs' feet and the sounds of chains being dragged across the floor. There were no dogs anywhere near the building, but it was well known that the lodge's original owner kept hunting dogs.

Now that Mallard Lodge has been abandoned once again, perhaps the ghosts have taken over the place entirely. Perhaps Murray is still on the job, busy keeping the lodge and the dogs in shape to receive guests. You never know, he might be hosting a visit from Clarke Gable and Cary Grant this very minute.

The Ghost of Henry Hudson

Canada's Indigenous Peoples have a rich heritage of folklore, but the earliest post-European contact ghost story I have been able to find west of the Maritimes was reported on February 21, 1878, in the *Manitoba Daily Free Press*. The event itself, however, had occurred more than two hundred and fifty years previously.

The story was reported to the *Free Press* from York Factory on the shores of Hudson Bay, after an employee of the Hudson's Bay Company was "searching among the archives of this old post and came upon a singular collection of relics." The newspaper article continues: "Perhaps the most interesting discovery [in the collection] is that of a . . . French manuscript, written in 1618 by one who signs himself, 'Louis Marin, mariner.'"

Marin had sailed in the ship *Discovery* with Henry Hudson on the leader's final failed attempt to find the Northwest Passage. *Discovery* set sail from England early in 1601. By June of that year, the beleaguered sailors had reached the shores of the bay now named for Hudson. The men camped there for some months but barely survived the following winter. By spring they were a dejected, disheartened lot, all of them desperately anxious to go back home.

But that spring, when the ice in the bay began to break up, Hudson announced that he had no intention of returning to England without first finding the elusive passage to the riches of the Orient. No longer able to trust their leader's ability to make wise judgements, the crew mutinied. Hudson, his son, and a number of crew members who had gone blind over the winter were set adrift in a small craft to face certain death. The mutineers immediately set sail back to England, sure they would never see Henry Hudson, his son, or the disabled sailors again.

But they were wrong. Marin wrote that during the entire voyage he was terrified for himself, the rest of the crew, and the *Discovery* itself because "every night at midnight the ghosts of the captain and the blind sailors came aboard and troubled us sorely."

Marin and his crewmates had survived the initial voyage across the Atlantic and lived through a winter when many of the sailors lost their sight due to poor diet only to be haunted by the apparitions of those they left behind.

If the ghosts of Hudson and his men still roam the frozen terrain near York Factory, they do so in peace by now, for that community, the earliest permanent European settlement in Manitoba, is now a ghost town. The post is preserved as a National Historic Site, but the area's harsh climate is taking its toll. The few remaining buildings, and even the land on which those buildings sit, are steadily crumbling. Soon the area will once again be as barren as it was when the crew from the *Discovery* sentenced its leader to death.

Historic Hamilton House

The tragic consequences of World War 1 followed by the worldwide flu epidemic in 1919 meant that, by the early 1920s, most families in North America, the United Kingdom, and Europe had been directly affected by at least one premature death. The emotional devastation the tragedies left in their wake was horrendous. The survivors feared their lives would never be complete again.

Perhaps it's not a coincidence, then, that a movement known as spiritualism became popular. Devotees of spiritualism actively sought communication with the dead by attending séances held in the homes of friends or neighbours, hoping for contact with a lost loved one. Any proof that the person they had lost still existed, albeit in another realm, was understandably comforting. Initially these sittings, as séances were sometimes called, were regarded as a novelty, but they grew to the status of a religion. Central Canada became a hotbed of the spiritualist movement.

Séances generally consisted of a few like-minded people sitting around a table in a darkened room. They either held hands or kept their hands on a small table in front of them to prevent any possibility of trickery. The group's leader was a medium, someone skilled at communication with the dead. The sittings, as the meetings were called, began with all the participants concentrating on contacting spirits.

When an entity responded, it either spoke through the medium or caused the table to levitate slightly and tap one leg on the floor in a code the group agreed upon. Usually one tap was understood to mean "yes," and two taps, "no" but this method could be enhanced with one tap for the letter "A," two taps for "B," and so on.

Dr. Samuel Aykroyd, a dentist based in rural Ontario, hosted many séances and left detailed accounts of all those events. His great-grandson, actor and comedian Dan Aykroyd, made good use of those records and wrote the movie *Ghostbusters*.

In Winnipeg, a respected family physician named Thomas Glendenning Hamilton was also intent on researching psychic phenomena. Dr. Hamilton became determined to scientifically prove whether or not communication with the dead was possible. He strove to keep his paranormal experiments as scientifically rigorous as possible. Toward that end, he invited a photographer to be present during the séances. After each session, he and the photographer would go directly into a darkroom where they developed the pictures. The results were impressive, often showing a disembodied head floating above the corporeal participants and occasionally even the image of an extra person, someone who hadn't been at the sitting.

These uncanny successes encouraged the group to continue with the photography. Some pictures captured images of objects flying through the air. The most interesting photos, however, illustrate the phenomenon of ectoplasm, a white fluid that manifested around a medium's head. This material often contained images of whatever spirit had been summoned. All of these photographs have been preserved and are kept at the University of Manitoba archives.

Dr. Hamilton's work soon earned him an international following. Prime Minister William Lyon Mackenzie King, Sir Arthur Conan Doyle, creator of the Sherlock Holmes mysteries, renowned physicist Sir Oliver Lodge, and other important figures of the day all attended meetings at Dr. Hamilton's Winnipeg home.

The soul of author Robert Louis Stevenson visited during one sitting. He assured the small audience that he was only one of the writers in the spirit world who wanted to assure the living that there is not only survival after death but that there could be communication between the two planes of existence.

The spirit of Frederic Myers, a deceased scholar and paranormal pioneer, also identified himself during a sitting, as did W.T. Stead, an English newspaper editor and enthusiastic psychic investigator whose life and research were cut short on April 14, 1912, when the doomed *Titanic* famously struck an iceberg.

Most spirit visitors to Hamilton's séances, however, were anonymous. One nameless spirit instructed the medium to get a pen and paper in order to receive this dictation: "The spirit world is the abode of undeveloped spirits, those who have not long left the body and those who by the law of the spirit life have not risen to higher spheres."

The entity also described his journey immediately after death by explaining, "I was taken into a mist like a great cloud which encircled me." Much to the disappointment of those attending the séance, the spirit added, "There is much superstition and bigotry on the subject of spirit communion among spirits as among those in the flesh."

By the mid-1930s, the excitement of spiritualism faded almost as quickly as it had begun and was replaced by the economic horrors of the Great Depression, when people's energies were diverted to the necessity of merely putting food on the table.

Even so, Dr. Hamilton was optimistic that enthusiasm for the movement would be rekindled. His hopes were not realized before his death in the spring of 1935. A few of those closest to Dr. Hamilton continued to hold séances after his death. Not surprisingly, the doctor's spirit attended some of those sessions himself.

The August 12, 1938, edition of the *Free Press* ran a small article about a former political colleague of Hamilton's who heard a familiar voice as he was attempting to communicate with spirits. It was

Hamilton with assurances that he was well and accompanied by his respected friend Sir Arthur Conan Doyle.

In January 1958, the *Free Press* ran a thirteen-part series about Dr. Hamilton's pioneering work. Margaret Hamilton, the paranormal pioneer's daughter, wrote the articles. In its introduction, the newspaper implied that the series would be something of a public service, providing background information about the paranormal. This indicates that people were still interested in the topic.

Although many of Hamilton's paranormal practices and results have been called into question since his death, no one can deny that he made a significant contribution to supernatural research in Canada.

And what of Hamilton's former home? Interestingly, it is apparently devoid of spirits, but perhaps that is only because there is no one left in the house to beckon them.

Dr. Hamilton's papers are kept at the University of Manitoba archives. Dr. Samuel Aykroyd's experiences have been documented by his grandson Peter H. Aykroyd in the book *The History of Ghosts, The True Story of Séances, Mediums, Ghosts and Ghostbusters*, which has a foreword by Dan Aykroyd.

The Grandfather Clock

Some ghosts haunt specific people, while others seem attached to certain places. But everyday objects can also be haunted. Sources of mechanical power, especially timepieces, for instance, are prone to being haunted and are often seen as an omen. The following story, which occurred in Winnipeg, Manitoba, is an example of this phenomenon, complete with a delightful twist.

The timepiece involved is a grandfather clock that had been a favoured possession of an elderly man named Walter. As the eldest son in his family, he had inherited the beautiful old clock from his father. He cherished it every day of his long life. When it seemed that Walter's time on earth was drawing to a close, his loved ones gathered around. They couldn't help but notice that as the dying man took his last breath, the pendulum on his treasured grandfather clock abruptly stopped swinging.

After Walter's funeral, members of the family took his old clock to be repaired. The clockmaker was a skilled craftsman, but he wasn't able to find any reason why the mechanism would have stopped working. Despite this, he wasn't able to get it to work again.

The family decided that, as there weren't any male heirs to pass the still and silent clock to, they would take it back to the man's house for his widow to enjoy as a piece of nostalgic furniture.

One day some years later, the woman returned home and was shocked to find the pendulum of the grandfather clock, which had been still for so long, swinging to and fro in its case, creating the familiar sound of loud ticking. As the woman stared at the clock in disbelief, her telephone rang. The voice on the other end of the line was that of her son-in-law. He was calling to tell her that her first grandson had been born just fifteen minutes before.

SASKATCHEWAN

The Haunted Hopkins Dining Parlour

The Hopkins Dining Parlour is one of Moose Jaw, Saskatchewan's most popular restaurants, and it's no wonder because the food and the service there are both excellent. It's the haunted ambience, though, that makes the parlour one of a kind.

The restaurant is named in honour of the original owners of the building: Edward and Minnie Hopkins. In the early days of the last century, Edward and Minnie were among the wealthiest citizens of Moose Jaw, and they built a home that reflected their status. The Hopkins lived in their mansion until they died in the 1930s. Then their daughter inherited the property. She found the place too big for her needs, so she converted several of the rooms into rental suites. Then in 1978, the Pierce family purchased the house, restored it to its former glory, and opened the Hopkins Dining Parlour. After that, it didn't take long for Gladys Pierce to realize that Edward and Minnie Hopkins hadn't, shall we say, entirely left the building.

Fortunately, Gladys was very accepting of the presences that haunted the place. Some of her employees, however, weren't so keen on the idea—at least not at first. When Brenda Wilson, who worked at the restaurant for thirty years, was first told about the resident ghosts, she thought that Gladys was just teasing her. By the time she realized that the ghost stories were no joke, she had become so fond of her job and her boss that she simply accepted the situation. Even so, when she left work at the end of a shift, Brenda made a point not to look back at the house because she'd heard that people had seen figures standing at the windows.

A couple that drove by the grand old house a few hours before the restaurant opened for the day stopped to take a picture. The following week, they made a point of going back while the place was open. They had something intriguing to show Gladys and Brenda. The photo they had taken a few days before when no one was in the restaurant included an image of a woman standing beside a small dog. The two figures were clear but ever so slightly transparent.

At least those spirits were serene and nonthreatening. Others are not. In the kitchen, for instance, workers have seen roasting pans mysteriously fly across the room. Cooks and their assistants have reported being tapped on their shoulders and have even felt their tense neck muscles massaged—all when there is no one near them. No one visible, that is.

Another employee stared in awe as a candleholder in a vacant room slowly moved side to side. In a different room, a candle on a dining room table sparked to life seemingly of its own volition.

Employees on the late shift are responsible for securing the restaurant, so it's understandable that they were concerned the night they heard party sounds coming from the floor above them, especially as they knew for a fact that there was no one upstairs at the time.

The staircase is one of the most haunted areas in the former mansion. People have reported seeing a child-sized cloud of mist drifting up the stairs, and an employee once watched a balloon float up the stairs, one at a time, until it reached the top and stopped.

And then there's the basement of the Hopkins Dining Parlour. People are never comfortable down there. They say they feel as though they are being watched. Some employees have been pushed, and others have heard the coin-rolling machine working when it was turned off. A new employee, who hadn't been told any of the ghost stories, reported seeing a faceless form moving in the darkened area.

The women's washroom is also an area that people say can feel "creepy." Brenda never forgot being in one of the stalls and hearing the sound of someone putting a paper towel into the garbage receptacle. She looked down at the opening under the stall door and saw a shadow. This puzzled her because she was sure the washroom had been empty when she'd come in only a few seconds before. Later a co-worker assured her that no one had gone into the room either before or after her.

And that wasn't an isolated event. Some women who've been touching up their lipstick in the washroom have felt as though something is about to grab at them, while others have watched the handles of the taps turn and water pour into the sink. Another customer was so certain she'd heard someone else had come into the ladies' room that she called out a greeting. When she didn't receive a reply, she came out of the stall and found herself standing in an otherwise empty room.

Staff calls one spirit "Minnie" in honour of Minnie Hopkins, the original lady of the house. Minnie's presence was confirmed when a witness said she recognized the ghostly face. The features were identical to that of the lady in the Hopkins' family photo.

Where ghosts are concerned, less can be more—more frightening that is. Take, for example, the server who saw just the hem of a skirt disappear around a corner. Similarly, a cook who arrived at work early one morning saw the hem of a skirt and a lady's shoe rounding another corner.

Minnie isn't alone in her afterlife. There is a gift shop in the Hopkins Dining Parlour where Gladys keeps items for customers who want a little something to take away from their visit. As luck would have it, one of those visitors was psychically sensitive. He saw the solid image of a man wearing an eyepatch. The encounter didn't upset the man because he was used to seeing spirits. He even assured Gladys that the ghost was not only harmless but only haunted one small section of the building.

Unfortunately, after that sighting, the man's ghost became more active and began roaming throughout the entire restaurant—and was seen by several members of the Hopkins' staff. The bartender reported that he often caught a glimpse of a man in the room, but when he turned to greet the person, there was no one there. A server watched as a figure walked in through the front door before disappearing out of sight. A cleaner once encountered the same ghost in an otherwise-empty restaurant. Despite the image's odd, old-fashioned clothes, the cleaner was so convinced that he was a real person that she even spoke to him. That was when the apparition vanished.

Not to be outdone, "Minnie" has remained as active as ever. One time, Brenda and two others were closing up the restaurant for the night. As they turned out all the lights, they noticed a single candle burning on one of the dining room tables. When they went into the room to investigate, all the lights in the restaurant came on. When one of the three saw an apparition standing between two tables, they all decided to leave the ghost alone in his haunt.

Children are generally more likely to be aware of ghosts. This was certainly the case when a little boy, no more than two years of age, stopped what he was doing and pointed at an apparently empty spot. "Ghost, ghost," he said. Brenda asked the child's father what his son was talking about, but the man had no idea. He said the boy hadn't learned to talk yet. Those were pretty dramatic first words.

When Gladys' granddaughter was four years old, she came to visit the restaurant. Brenda saw the child sitting at a table and watched as a shiver ran through the child. When she asked the girl what the matter was, she informed Brenda that "a ghost had just gone by."

"I said, 'like Casper?'" Brenda remembers. "She said, 'No, a lady ghost.'"

That "lady ghost" was likely implicated in another sighting that Brenda recalls. Two older women brought a little girl with them for a special lunch. Brenda stopped by the table to talk with the trio. As she chatted, she noticed that the girl was extremely quiet and had barely touched her food. Two days later, she learned that the child had seen a lady wearing a white dress with a yellow apron. The image was leaning against a buffet, smiling. The girl said she had been scared because she could tell that the smiling woman was not of this world.

Once a worker was upset by a presence she saw while she was setting up tables after the restaurant had closed. She had come down from the third floor to the second and was about to go back up when she stopped cold. The silverware that she had just set out on the tables had moved to the stairs where it was elaborately laid out in the shape of a cross. The next morning, the witness and a friend came back into the restaurant and both saw the image of a lady with long white hair sitting at a table.

When electrical appliances and telephones malfunction at the restaurant, the employees just blame the ghosts and get on with their day as best they can. They've learned that once the paranormal activity settles down again all will be back to normal. Even so, it can be a challenge. Brenda remembers one day when a customer said to her, "there's a lot of activity [here]." Brenda agreed that it was a busy day, but the woman shook her head and clarified her observation. She had meant there was a lot of *spiritual* activity. Brenda simply nodded. By then she and the others had adapted to working in a haunted house. They knew this was just business as usual at the Hopkins Dining Parlour.

Sadly, Brenda Wilson passed away while this book was being compiled. She is greatly missed by all who knew her.

Echoes of the Past

The Echo Valley Conference Centre, just north of Fort Qu'Appelle, Saskatchewan, stands near the shores of Echo Lake. The enormous property is in a picturesque setting and dotted with charmingly restored historical buildings. The centre is a popular venue for conferences and retreats as well as weddings and other celebrations. All of this is quite a change from the facility's atmosphere when it opened in 1919. Then called "Fort San," it was a place to be dreaded: it was a tuberculosis sanatorium.

Tuberculosis was a death threat until the mid-1940s and the advent of antibiotic drugs. As medical science honed these new drugs, the number of tuberculosis cases decreased rapidly, allowing Fort San and many other sanatoriums to begin closing their wards.

In 1972, the government of Saskatchewan bought the sprawling property for one dollar. Despite the low price, the place was not a good real estate investment because it no longer served any purpose and was very expensive to maintain. Before long, the once-proud buildings were so rundown that they were a danger. Finally, the Western Canadian Sea Cadet Training Program moved to the site and provided enough cash flow to support the property's necessary remediation. These were the first steps toward a new life for the place that once meant death.

Today the old hospital is a popular venue known as the Echo Valley Conference Centre. Nostalgia buffs enjoy exploring the well-maintained grounds and old-fashioned buildings. Not surprisingly, ghostly legends have grown up around the facility, with some psychically sensitive folks claiming to have seen the spirits of former patients shuffling along in certain corridors.

A musician attending a band camp at the centre settled in to rehearse with his bandmates when he realized that he needed to get something from his room. He excused himself and hurried back to the dorm. As he stood in his room, he heard a woman singing. This struck him as very odd because this was the men's quarters. Still, he couldn't deny what he'd heard. Quietly, he stepped into the hallway and realized the voice was coming from a nearby washroom. He peeked around the corner and saw a woman wearing an old-fashioned dress standing at one of the sinks and singing while she washed her hands. The faucet was turned on, and water streamed into the sink. The man called out hesitantly to let her know that she was in the wrong building, but the singer didn't seem to hear him. He called again, and this time the apparition moved farther away from him until her image vanished completely.

The young man wasn't frightened, but he was extremely puzzled. He stood beside the sink where he'd seen the figure and wondered where she could have gone. Then he turned toward the sink and realized the porcelain was bone dry; there couldn't have been water pouring into it only a moment before. But he knew what he had seen, and that frightened him enough that he made a point never to be alone in that building again.

Over the years, various writers' groups have spent time at Echo Valley, and some have come away with more than just completed manuscripts. Many of the attendees knew about the former sanatorium's haunted reputation, and one evening a foolhardy wordsmith brought a Ouija board into a common room. By now there are a number of variations of the events that took place after, but there is one central theme to all the accounts: fright. Such fright that not one of those involved in the attempted séance ventured back to their rooms that night. Instead, they all spent an uncomfortable night on chairs in the common room, preferring the security of one another's company to the isolation of their single rooms. Judging by how many writers have shared that story, it seems safe to say that everyone lived through the encounter—despite the heavy toll on their nervous systems.

Of course, those writers were only in one building and for just a few days. A woman named Bernice had a lifelong connection with Fort San. As a child, Bernice was a patient when the facility was a sanatorium. As an adult, she worked at the conference centre.

Fortunately, Bernice didn't know anything about the ghost stories when she was a young patient at the sanatorium. It wasn't until she came to work there as an adult that she encountered revenants from years before. She's heard footfalls in empty hallways, furniture being dragged across empty rooms, and doors slamming closed. At first Bernice assumed that the noises came from another area of the building, but when she checked with her co-workers she was shocked to find out that they had heard the noises too but had presumed she was the one making the commotion.

And then there's Nurse Jane. Jane is a nurse who worked at the sanatorium and is rumoured to have committed suicide. To this day, it's said that her image can still be seen both in and outside of the buildings. Her spirit has also become known as Folding Nurse Jane because when her ghost is seen inside she seems to be folding sheets and towels. Those who see her outside on the grounds say that she's pushing a wheelchair—no word on whether or not that wheelchair is occupied.

A wheelchair figures in another unexplained sighting. In this case it's only a shadow, though, a shadow of a nonexistent wheelchair.

More recently, an employee at the conference centre found an old-fashioned nurse's cap. She asked around, and no one seemed to know anything about it, so she took the souvenir home with her. The next day, however, she brought the piece of nostalgia back. It seems that something about the white starched cap utterly terrified her. She never shared the details of her experience but just tucked the hat away where she had found it. The next day the cap was gone. Had Folding Nurse Jane reclaimed what was rightfully hers?

Once a cleaner, working in a building that has since been torn down, noted that some hallway lights had been left on, and she turned them off. Moments later the lights came on again. She figured that if something beyond our world wanted those lights left on, then she would happily oblige. It's no surprise that she and many other cleaners much preferred to work in pairs.

The staff at the Echo Valley Conference Centre is ready to welcome guests and equipped to meet all their needs. Spirits are optional!

A Dark and Evil Presence

Weyburn is a pretty city in southeastern Saskatchewan. In 1919, construction began on an enormous institution, the "Weyburn Mental Hospital." With its opening, the city's future changed forever because, for decades, the hospital was the area's largest employer. Patients admitted there were offered the most advanced therapies of the era. Sadly, in those days little was known about mental illnesses, and the treatments were barbaric: physical restraints, baths of scalding or icy water, forced labour, and experimental drugs.

In 1971, most of the "mental patients," as they were then called, had been dispersed to other establishments, and parts of the old hospital were repurposed as a smaller, extended care facility or, as many claimed, a haunted extended care facility. All the human drama and suffering that had played out within those walls left behind both visual and auditory remnants.

During this transition, the floors were closed down one at a time. Many of those who worked on the project had strange tales to tell. Some were sure that they overheard muffled conversations echoing through the stairwells. When this happened, someone always checked to see who had come in. But those stairwells were always empty. Others reported hearing footsteps along the corridors where no human was stirring.

At night, people swore they could see the silhouette of a woman standing at a darkened window—when they knew no one was in that part of the building.

Small pieces of jewellery or coins or other small mementoes often feature in a haunting, and this was the case at the Weyburn hospital. Staff would occasionally find a ring in the middle of an empty room. Wisely, no one ever picked the trinket up, but even so, the next time they looked, there was nothing on the floor—until the next time.

Other more stationary artefacts were a curator's responsibility. Unfortunately, the woman assigned to the job happened to be psychically sensitive. She enjoyed her work, even when it was a challenge for her to process all the leftover psychic energy around her, which she described as "humming like a beehive."

Employees with similar sensitivities described feeling people rushing along empty hallways and even heard voices calling out to them. Most others simply felt that they were never alone when they worked and that they were always being watched.

When a group of paranormal researchers, all used to being in haunted buildings, went into the empty old hospital, they sensed a dark and evil presence surrounding them. They staunchly maintained that touring the mammoth building that had once been the Weyburn Mental Hospital was the most frightening task they had ever carried out.

In 2009, crews finally began demolishing the massive old structure that had been abandoned and boarded up since 2006. The process was a long and arduous one, beginning with months of remediation work. Their efforts were successful. It seems that the dark, unnatural energy that haunted the place all those years has finally dispersed.

Phantom Train

As all Canadian school children know, Canada's railway has linked the country from east to west since 1885. It's no wonder, then, that we have our share of phantom train stories. Most of these tales are merely recollections by now, but there's an apparition near the town of St. Louis, Saskatchewan (130 kilometres northeast of Saskatoon) that rarely disappoints. Train buffs say that judging by the phantom locomotive's distinctive headlight, the engine dates back to the days of steam power, so today there's no mistaking the ghost light for an actual train—especially as the tracks this train runs on were ripped up years ago. It's as if time has stopped on this small stretch of land and has remained stopped for nearly a hundred years.

Like many ghost stories, the origins of this tale are not for the faint of heart. Most versions of the legend involve the gruesome accidental death of a railway employee. Some say he was an engineer or a conductor. Other witnesses, those who see a small red light near the large white one, are sure that the poor soul was a track worker responsible for holding up a red lantern as a signal for an oncoming train to switch tracks. If this is the case, then his presence is apparently doomed to spend his afterlife walking beside nonexistent railway tracks, futilely warning engineers of impending disaster.

Whatever the details may have been, the legend is amazingly consistent and very well accepted. The spectral lights run through farmland and follow the route where the track once lay. The story has been handed down from parents and grandparents; hundreds of people, including a former mayor of St. Louis, have reported personal encounters.

Not surprisingly, many of those who've waited for a sighting are young men in their teens and early twenties. Two of those were Edmonton film-school students Kim and Derek. They chose to make a documentary film about ghosts in Western Canada, and so it was that on a cold January evening they set out in a small, ageing car and headed east to Saskatchewan. They drove straight through and arrived, as planned, just at midnight. Despite the cold, both of them were anxious to get out of the car to stretch their legs. They stepped out and scanned their surroundings.

"I wonder what the light will look like?" Kim asked rhetorically.

"Just like that!" Derek replied excitedly, pointing to a spot roughly 15 metres from where they stood.

Derek was correct. They were staring at the famous St. Louis light. Sadly, their timing could have been better. Their camera equipment was still in the car, and by the time they managed to get it set up, the light was gone. All they came away with was a story to tell their grandchildren.

Another group of young men had to be more patient than Kim and Derek, but they were finally rewarded with a sighting. The light appeared off in the distance and glowed for a remarkably long time, never seeming to move closer or farther away. The friends decided to do an experiment; they drove their car along a dirt path beside the old track bed, toward the apparition. They had only driven a few metres when suddenly the light in the distance vanished completely, but the interior of their car glowed as though it was daylight. Terrified, they jumped out of the car and saw that the light was shining again, but from behind them now. It would seem from their experience that the light does, indeed, move.

A young man named Chris grew up in Prince Albert, just a short drive north of St. Louis. When he was in high school, Chris often enjoyed an inexpensive evening's entertainment by driving out to see the ghost train with his friends. As their visits became more frequent, their courage, or foolishness, also increased.

"One of the unwritten rules of the St. Louis light is that you never park your car on the track bed. Being the immortal adolescent that I was, I sometimes did just that," Chris recalls. This act of defiance produced a variety of small problems. Sometimes the car's windshield wipers would turn on spontaneously, or the headlights would flicker on and off. Other times it would be difficult to restart the engine.

One winter night, Chris and a friend drove out to see the light. They parked their car where the tracks once were and, perhaps anticipating that it might be troublesome to restart it, they left the engine running. "We didn't have to wait long," says Chris of seeing the apparition. "The train showed up after about two minutes."

The teens only watched the approaching light for a few seconds, however, before something else captured their attention: steam seemed to be billowing out from under their car's hood. Thinking that the radiator had boiled over, they shut off the ignition and hurried out to take a look at the engine. One deep breath told them that it wasn't steam they were dealing with. This was smoke, and the cause appeared to be a fire in the alternator.

"We had no way of extinguishing an electrical fire, so we decided to blow it out on the highway," Chris explains. They made the return trip as fast as they dared. Even though the car ran like a charm, all the way home, they had a mechanic take a look under the hood. The man admitted that he could not figure out what might have happened to cause the smoke. Chris had heard of other people who'd experienced car trouble near the track bed. Sometimes cars wouldn't start. Other times the radio would turn on or off suddenly.

Chris's experiences happened many years ago, but he remains fascinated by the St. Louis light to this day. "I have heard scientific explanations for the ghost light, and someday I would like to try to prove these theories."

Fellow ghost-story author Shannon Sinn (*The Haunting of Vancouver Island*) grew up in Prince Albert, Saskatchewan. He has seen the ghost light many times and says that "whole groups of people have seen it at the same time."

There have been frequent attempts by photographers, both amateur and professional, to capture a photograph of the apparition. The results have been interesting, if not conclusive. In one case, an entire film turned out blank with the exception of two small red dots that were described as looking like "eyes."

Not everyone believes the legend of the phantom train. There are skeptics too. A volunteer with the Prince Albert Historical Museum once used his camera equipment to debunk the theory of the phantom light. In the February 29, 1992, edition of the *Prince Albert Daily Herald*, he explained his idea in a letter to the editor. "The lights are vehicle lights that appear and then disappear owing to the changes in the elevation of the highway. They are plainly visible with a high-power telephoto lens or a good field glass."

Others disagree with that theory, claiming to have tested it by flashing car lights at various points on the highway and recording the appearance of these lights by the track. The conclusion, they say, was that the tiny distant headlights bore no resemblance at all to the huge white beacon that so many have witnessed.

A man whose ancestors have lived in the St. Louis area for years also addressed the possibility of vehicle lights as a source of the mystery. He told a reporter with the *Prince Albert Daily Herald* that his great-grandmother remembers people talking about the light when she was a teenager. There were almost no cars in the area at that time. Another long-standing member of the community once said simply, "That train came around that bend so many times, it probably wore a groove into something." Students of the paranormal would call that a psychic imprint.

Whatever the explanation behind the St. Louis ghost train might be, there is definitely something to this multigenerational mystery.

Bess

The Delta Bessborough Hotel in Saskatoon, fondly known as "Bess," is a dignified old structure. It is only fitting that a dignified old ghost haunts it. They call him the Man in Grey. Legend has it that, in life, the man worked at the hotel. He was known as a pleasant person who was always impeccably dressed.

When he was at the front desk one night, the switchboard received a call from a guest about a rowdy party going on a few doors down the hall. Never one to shirk his responsibilities, the loyal employee went up to the party room, knocked on the door, and asked that the partiers keep the noise down. Those were the last words the man ever uttered—alive, that is. The two men who answered the door picked him up and threw him over the railing to the foyer below.

The well-dressed man did not survive the fall, except in spirit. His image is still seen strolling through the Bess. He's always dressed in a perfectly fitted grey suit and witnesses consistently note that he is tall and slim but not very ghost-like. The Man in Grey is not slightly transparent, as many ghosts are, but solid. Occasionally he'll greet a passerby with a nod and a friendly, "hello," but other than that he simply goes about his afterlife, looking very natty and not disturbing a soul. He's just the ghost the Bessborough Hotel deserves.

Darke Hall

Sometimes it can be difficult to figure out why a particular place is haunted, or who the ghost might be. That is not the case at the Darke Hall, once known as the Music and Art Building, on the University of Regina campus in Regina, Saskatchewan.

Francis Darke was a successful business owner, philanthropist, and the former mayor of Regina. In 1928, Darke donated $125,000 dollars to have a grand concert hall built in his beloved city. The hall still stands, and the citizens of Regina are still passionate and generous in supporting its existence—even Darke himself. The man died in 1940, but his recognizable image is frequently seen sitting in the audience during performances. His spectre sits alone, nattily dressed in formal old-fashioned clothing.

Performers who catch a glimpse of him are understandably startled because it's apparently very obvious that the image is not from this world. Some of the people who work in the auditorium have taken to greeting Mr. Darke as they arrive in the morning. Others have seen his image standing outside on the steps of the building named in his honour.

ALBERTA

Haunted Quarters

The word "poltergeist" is German for "noisy ghost," and it's a term that is used to describe an entity that makes its presence known by knocking on walls, touching people, and even through telekinesis, which is making objects move, seemingly on their own.

The following true story is a dramatic example of a poltergeist haunting. The people involved have asked to remain anonymous, so their names are altered slightly.

When Don Miller, an armed forces search-and-rescue technician, was transferred to Edmonton, Alberta, he and his wife, Bobbie, along with their infant son, were assigned a house on the military base. As it turned out, this was a house they would never forget, but they've only recently been able to talk about their experiences.

"We kept the accounting pretty well to ourselves. The armed forces takes a dim view of its personnel seeing ghosts and then coming to work," Don explains.

The Millers had two pets, a large mutt named Misty and a black cat named Willow. The animals were the first to realize that something was seriously amiss in their new home, while Don and Bobbie slipped straight into denial.

"At first it was always little things, and we made excuses," Don says. "We had a dream catcher hanging in a corner of the living room. The dog and the cat would sit motionless for hours staring at that loop."

Soon the dream catcher began spinning even when there was no air movement in the living room. Worse, although it was only turning in one direction, the line on which it hung never shortened.

"Sometimes it would spin very fast, absolutely go crazy," Bobbie remembers. She had no idea that the ornament's activity was her introduction to life with an amazingly vigorous phantom.

"There never seemed to be any malevolence," the couple concurs. "These were more childish, attention-getting behaviours."

The entity's next target was a common toy for poltergeists: the television set.

"It was a very old television. The channel selector was the old rotary type. It didn't turn easily," Don explains, adding that the dial was so stiff it made more of a clunk than a click.

One evening, as Don sat enjoying a television show, the channel selector suddenly turned to another setting. Annoyed by the disruption, Don got up and switched the knob back to where it had been. He was puzzled but not concerned, and he didn't share his experience with Bobbie for another few days. By then the channel changing had become annoyingly frequent.

After a few sessions of unwanted channel surfing and a spinning dream catcher, the couple began to discuss the strange events they'd each noted but never mentioned.

"It happens all the time," Bobbie responded when Don told her about his experience with the television dial.

"Bobbie was comfortable with the whole thing," Don says. "I wasn't. I wasn't scared by it; I just wasn't very comfortable. The next time the dial on the television moved, I yelled at it and said that I owned the television and to leave it alone."

As he watched, the dial moved back to where it had been, but from that point on "There was always something," Bobbie says.

There were two bedrooms in the house, both on the second floor. "We used the room across from our bedroom as a combination spare room, storage, sewing, and utility room," Don says. One reason that room was chosen as the spare room was that it always felt cold. Neither of the Miller's pets would go into that room, but it was one of the ghost's favourite places.

"We kept photo albums in that room. Two pictures from the albums began turning up on the guest bed in that room," Bobbie explains, before adding that no one else had been upstairs in their home. She asked Don if he'd taken the pictures out. When he told her he hadn't, she simply put the photos back where they belonged. They didn't stay there very long. After the same two pictures had appeared on the bed several times, Bobbie was convinced that Don was playing a practical joke on her. She was annoyed and took the incident up with her husband.

He attests, "I knew I wasn't doing it, so I told Bobbie to wait until I was out one day and then hide the photographs somewhere. That way if they reappeared, she'd know that I had nothing to do with it. Sure enough, two days later, there they were on the bed, always the same ones."

The Millers kept a heavy old Underwood typewriter in that room. It sat on top of an antique sewing machine cabinet.

"One day I walked past the doorway to the spare room and there was the typewriter . . . on the floor," Bobbie remembers. There was certainly no way a machine weighing more than ten kilograms could have fallen without someone hearing it. Besides, it's doubtful that the machine would have landed in such a nice, neat, upright position right beside the sewing machine. Not knowing what else to do, the woman lifted the old typewriter back onto the cabinet. At the time, she could not have imagined the encounters she was destined to have with the old machine.

The dream catcher still spun frequently for no apparent reason, and the family pets still stared intently in that direction for hours. Willow, the cat, however, would also stare into the spare room in much the same way. The dog's reaction was even more dramatic. Despite the fact that Misty was a well-trained and normally obedient dog, she absolutely refused to enter the spare room, no matter how much she was coaxed or ordered to. Both animals clearly sensed there was something unnatural in there.

It seemed that just as Don and Bobbie became adjusted to each of the spirit's hijinks, the entity added another trick to its repertoire. One morning, as Don stood at the top of the stairs looking down, he saw what he thinks might have been their resident presence.

"She was standing at the bottom of the stairs. She was slender and had shoulder-length hair. She wore a dark dress with flowers," he recalls. Utterly astonished by what he was seeing, he wanted to share the experience with Bobbie, and yet, "I had the sense that if I turned away the ghost wouldn't be there when I turned back."

He was correct, the ghost disappeared, but his convictions about what he saw never wavered. "I stand by what I saw," the no-nonsense man states firmly.

Given the seeming contradiction between the image Don saw and the type of ghostly activity they had been experiencing, it's possible that the apparition at the bottom of the stairs was another, more passive spirit. She may have been in the house all along, or she may have just been passing through that one morning.

Bobbie made a habit of glancing into the spare room each time she passed it. Whenever she found the typewriter on the floor, she would calmly put it back up onto the sewing-machine cabinet. One day, while going about her chores on the main floor of the house, she heard the readily identifiable sound of typing coming from upstairs. That was enough. She lugged the heavy old thing down to the basement and set it on the floor. At least there it couldn't fall again. The relocation, however, didn't stop the sounds of typing.

A few weeks later, while listening to the typewriter keys tapping away rhythmically downstairs, Bobbie had an idea. When all was quiet, she went into the basement and rolled a fresh piece of paper into the typewriter. Oddly, it seemed that inserting the paper stopped the entity's interest in the typewriter—at first anyway.

The Millers' haunted house was quiet for a while. Then, when Bobbie came downstairs to make breakfast one morning, a sight greeted her that she will never forget. Each knife, fork, and spoon in the kitchen drawer was bent in half. Every piece of cutlery. Bobbie ordered the spirit to repair the damage it had done. Then she went back upstairs. When she returned to the kitchen, the cutlery had been straightened.

Don and Bobbie thought they were resigned to the spirit's hijinks until the day Bobbie's mother called and invited the young family for dinner. Pleased, Bobbie returned to her day's routine. Not long afterward, she heard a noise coming from the basement. It was the typewriter.

Revealing her admirably calm and accepting nature, Bobbie waited until the sounds stopped and then went down to the basement. Her foresight with the sheet of paper had finally paid off. The spirit had left a message. Full of anticipation, she pulled the sheet from the roller only to discover that she was not dealing with a deeply philosophical ghost. There, where all the answers to this world's great unknown could have been revealed, was this simple message: HAVE A PLEASANT TIME AT YOUR PARENTS' HOME.

She was understandably unnerved to have received a direct message from the beyond, but her overriding feeling was one of frustration at the message's mundane content. It seemed nothing more than the ghostly equivalent of the standard, and virtually meaningless, "Have a nice day."

Although Bobbie never left paper in the typewriter again, she and Don both continued to hear the keys being depressed as the machine sat, unattended, on the floor in their basement.

Throughout all these events, Bobbie went about her life as normally as possible. "In a strange way it was company for me," she recalls.

But the persistent spirit was about to go too far.

"One afternoon I put the baby down for his nap. He was about six months old at the time. A couple of hours later, I heard him waking up and went upstairs to get him out of his crib." She only got as far as the bedroom doorway because there, stacked neatly on top of the child's dresser, stood every article of clothing the baby owned. When she had put him into his crib earlier in the afternoon, his clothes had been in the drawers where they belonged.

A supernatural being with an interest in her child was more than Bobbie could bear. She was ready to look for a new house. Don, who had never been as easygoing as his wife about living in a haunted house, concurred immediately and, using the ruse of needing a roomier place, began to inquire about vacant houses on the base. Within a short time, they moved to the new place.

At the time of writing, the haunted dwelling is still standing and apparently occupied, but the Millers, who are no longer associated with the military and no longer live in Edmonton, haven't bothered to enquire whether their old home is still haunted by an energetic poltergeist. They're just content that the ghost did not follow them.

The Banff Springs Hotel

Sir William Cornelius Van Horne (1843–1915) was the man largely responsible for completing the railway that links Canada from coast to coast. Van Horne was also our country's original marketing guru. When he first set eyes on the majestic Rocky Mountains, he declared, "If we can't export the scenery, we'll have to import the tourists." Van Horne's idea was extra canny because those tourists would have to travel to the mountains on the newly completed railway.

Once the train had dropped the travellers off amid the majesty of the Rocky Mountains, the tourists would, of course, need a place to stay. Van Horne had another innovative idea, and construction on the Banff Springs Hotel began in 1887. A year later, the hotel welcomed its first guests. The original building was humble compared to today's palatial resort, but it was enormously popular nevertheless.

The Banff Springs Hotel has since been rebuilt and renovated many times, but the lavish hotel still stands nestled at the base of Sulphur Mountain, tucked in the coniferous forest of Banff National Park in

Alberta. Even today, some fortunate people stay for prolonged visits, as was the custom more than a hundred years ago. Others never leave. And who can blame them? What a magnificent place to spend eternity.

The Dancing Bride is one of the hotel's best-known ghosts. Late at night, when the lights have dimmed and most of the guests have gone to their luxurious rooms, a vaporous column of mist occasionally forms at the base of a grandly curving staircase. Some witnesses say that the mist disappears again in the blink of an eye; others maintain that as the moments pass, the cloud becomes more solid until they realize they are staring at the unmistakable image of a young woman dressed in a long flowing white bridal gown. She seems to be hovering just above the floor, and she glides effortlessly in a three-step pattern that repeats itself over and over again, until finally the glistening speckles of white light disperse, and the spectre vanishes completely—until the next time.

In life, the bride and her groom chose the Banff Springs Hotel as the perfect setting for their fairy-tale wedding. The bride made her entrance at the top of a curving staircase with each stair subtly lit by the glow of a small candle. The effect could not have been more romantic. But then disaster struck. The long, flowing train of the bride's gown brushed up against one of those candles, and the delicate material caught fire. When she realized what had happened, the bride panicked, lost her balance, and fell to the bottom of the staircase. She died instantly, but her spirit has lingered for many decades. People who have seen the image say she appears to be made of glistening speckles of white light. She glides along repeating the same three-step pattern over and over again. It seems that the bride's ethereal, slightly transparent image eternally dances the wedding waltz that she wasn't able to enjoy in life.

And then there's the ghost of Sam Macauley. Sam emigrated from Scotland and worked as bellman at the Banff Springs Hotel for some forty years. Sam always said that, when he died, he would come back to haunt the hotel; according to many eyewitness accounts, he has done exactly that. One of the devoted soul's most famous appearances occurred back in the late 1970s, when a family checked into the hotel late in the evening. They were tired from their travels and thankful when an older man dressed in an old-fashioned uniform helped carry their luggage to their room.

The next morning, they realized that they had all been so tired the night before that none of them had thought to tip the kindly man with the distinctive brogue. Before they went out for their first day of exploring, they stopped at the front desk and asked about the dignified older bellman.

The clerk at the desk looked puzzled and told the family there wasn't a bellman at the Banff Springs over the age of thirty. Then it was the guests' turn to look puzzled. They insisted that the man who had helped them the previous evening was considerably older than thirty. They added that he was dressed in an old-fashioned uniform and spoke with a Scottish brogue.

The clerk's face went pale. They were describing Sam Macauley, and he had been dead for more than a year.

Sam's spirit is an active one. Staff members blame him for elevators that go up and down when no one's in them. It's thought that Sam is checking on the cache of tip money that he was rumoured to have hidden away somewhere in the hotel. True to form, during a reception to launch a television series about haunted places in Canada in the 1990s, the elevators closest to the reception room were active all evening—and no one was near them.

There are also other, less well-known, spirits haunting the Banff Springs Hotel. One is an apparition of a little girl bouncing a ball in a corridor. The child runs toward the end of the hallway only to vanish just as she reaches the end. No one knows who she was in life or why her ghost haunts this particular corridor, but that's the thing about ghosts: they defy human logic. There's also a ghostly bartender who admonishes patrons who have had too much to drink! Seeing him should scare almost anyone sober.

Happily, in addition to the resort's other fine qualities, the Banff Springs Hotel embraces its status as one of Canada's most haunted places. If you visit Banff, don't pass up the opportunity to enjoy this haunted castle in the woods.

The Bruin Inn

For more than seventy years, the Bruin Inn was a popular place to quench one's thirst. Located in the heart of St. Albert, Alberta, a community just north of Edmonton, the inn's California Mission-style architecture made it look oddly out of place in north-central Alberta since the day it was built.

That incongruity became decidedly more pronounced over the years as St. Albert became more upscale while the inn aged gracelessly and became rundown. Finally, in the summer of 2000, a wrecking crew moved in to reduce the historic old watering hole to a pile of rubble. Hundreds of townsfolk turned out to watch the demolition; some said they could almost see the history of the seedy old place billowing up from the rubble.

The Bruin Inn's early days were anchored in simpler times. Prohibition laws had just been overturned, finally freeing Albertans to quaff an alcoholic beverage legally. But the destitution of the Dirty Thirties had just begun. It was in this setting that lawmakers saw potential problems brewing. Men who were drinking, it seemed, tended to start fights, and these altercations often began as disputes over the perceived or real attentions of women. The authorities were confident that segregation would solve the issue. Men and women simply must not drink together. Men must drink in one room and women in another.

But, interestingly, that ruling only held in the cities of Calgary and Edmonton. Away from those two metropolises, men, even when drinking, could apparently be counted upon to act as gentlemen when women were around.

Many ramifications flowed from there, but the most important one for the Bruin Inn was that, owing to its proximity to Edmonton, it became a popular and profitable business, attracting city couples who understandably wished to share a beverage in the same room.

It's thought to be around this time that the inn first became haunted. No one knew who the ghost might have been when she was alive or why she haunted the place, but anyone who ever saw her described the spirit of a woman dressed in clothing from the 1930s. She floated along the upstairs corridor, and then, as she made her ghostly rounds, the misty figure would always stop at one particular window and gaze down toward the street, much to the amazement of the earthly folks strolling along the sidewalk below.

The second ghost in the Bruin was the spirit of an old man. It is said that he had died in the bar while listening to a fellow drinker's tall tale. Apparently, when the storyteller came to the punch line of his anecdote, he slapped his hand down on the table for emphasis. The elderly chap was so startled by the sudden action that he suffered a fatal heart attack. His spirit was usually seen in the guest room located directly above the inn's front doors.

For three years prior to its demolition, the Bruin Inn stood vacant. It's likely that both of the ghosts remained happily in residence for that time because at least one theory holds that ghosts prefer, and even flourish in, empty buildings. If that theory is true, in the case of St. Albert's haunted and abandoned Bruin Inn, then the demolition must have been the saddest surprise of the ghosts' afterlives. We can only hope they've happily found other haunts.

The Man in Black

Albert Earnest Cross, one of the founders of the Calgary Stampede, died in 1932, but his legacy lives on, not only in the world-famous stampede but also in the following ghost story. For understandable reasons, the man who had this extraordinary encounter has asked that his name be altered to protect his anonymity.

In 1967, Canada's centennial year, Richard Wilson lived in Calgary, Alberta, and worked part-time as a cab driver to help support his young family. He soon learned to be at certain addresses at certain times in order to get the best fares. One of those choice spots was the York Hotel at closing time. And so it was that on a lovely spring evening, Wilson parked his car in line for what cab drivers called "the beer rush."

The first customer to come out of the hotel walked straight to Wilson's car and got in. He was dressed in black from head to toe, and he was absolutely silent. This didn't bother the part-time driver because he knew that some passengers simply chose not to talk. Wilson remembers that the man in black simply pointed "and somehow I knew where he wanted to go."

A few minutes later, the cab driver pulled his car to the curb. The silent man paid his fare, got out, and started walking toward a large house. The driver watched for a moment, then he put the money away. When he looked up again, the man in black was gone; presumably he was already in the house. Wilson drove away to finish his night's work.

When Wilson tallied up the fares at the end of his shift, he found he was short by exactly the amount the silent man in black had paid him. How could that be? Wilson was good with numbers and always balanced his books to the penny. This time, however, no matter how many times he recalculated the figures, he came out short by the same amount of money. Finally, he gave up and had to accept that somehow he'd been shorted.

Fortunately, life wasn't all work for Wilson and his family that year. There were special events all over the country for Canada's one-hundredth birthday, and the Wilsons took in as many as they could.

They visited the Horseman's Hall of Fame, which had an exhibit featuring the founders of the Calgary Stampede, including photos.

One of those was of A. E. Cross. Wilson recognized him instantly; he told his family that he had driven the man home one evening. Wilson's wife was taken aback because the man's date of death was recorded just below his picture. Cross died in 1932, long before Wilson was even born.

Wilson was astonished. He clearly recalled that silent man in black. Now that he thought more about the passenger, he realized that the stranger had looked "too clean, too perfect, like someone had made him up for television." In the spring of 1967, Richard Wilson had taken a ghost for a drive.

How Medicine Hat Came to Have Its Name

Medicine Hat, Alberta, stands on the banks of the picturesque South Saskatchewan River. The city as it is known today began life in 1883, when crews from the Canadian Pacific Railway arrived in the area to build a railroad bridge. Prior to that, the land had been home to the Blackfoot people for thousands of years; the city's name is a tribute to a supernatural legend held sacred by the Blackfoot.

The words "medicine hat" are an English translation of the Blackfoot word *Saamis*. There are variations on how this came to be the city's name, but the most widely accepted version of the legend originated centuries ago during a harsh winter when the Blackfoot people were dying from cold and starvation. The hardships were so severe that something had to be done, or there would be no one still alive come spring.

Toward this end, the elders convened and decided they would send one of their strongest and bravest young men in search of a solution. The chosen one, his wife, and their wolf dog walked along the frozen South Saskatchewan River until they came to a particular opening in the river's ice. The spot was sacred to their people because they believed that the water spirits went there to breathe.

The couple and the dog struggled to make an overnight camp as the cold, cruel winter winds blew around them. By morning, after very little sleep, the pair set about summoning the spirits. Soon a serpent rose through the hole in the ice, and the man explained their people's situation. The creature listened and then demanded a sacrifice: the man's much-loved wife. In return, the serpent promised to give the man a headdress called a *Saamis* that would make its owner all-powerful.

Horrified at the thought of his beautiful young wife dying, the husband tried to trick the spirit by throwing his dog into the river instead. The substitute did not please the serpent. Heartsick, the man did not know what to do. He loved his wife dearly, but he also knew that he was responsible for the survival of his people. Finally, with his heart breaking, he threw his wife into the frigid river and to certain death.

After a time, the serpent reappeared and told the young man to spend the night on a nearby island and then to go to the base of the great cliffs at sunrise. There he would find a powerful headdress known as a "medicine hat" or *Saamis*.

The brave man followed the apparition's directions and found the mystical hat. He put it on and soon after found the food that saved his people from starvation.

As the years went by, the Blackfoot flourished, and because he possessed the *Saamis*, the brave and obedient man rose to become an esteemed leader.

And that, according to legend, is how the city of Medicine Hat came to have its unusual name. The legend is so important to the city that it is told in a beautiful brick mural at the civic centre.

Medicine Hat's Phantom Train

The story of Medicine Hat's ghost train is ingrained in the city's history. You would be hard-pressed to find a resident of the southeastern Alberta city who does not know the terrible and mysterious legend.

One fine evening in late spring of 1908, Bob Twohey and Gus Day reported for work at the Canadian Pacific Railroad rail yards. Bob was an engineer, and Gus was a stoker. They were assigned to take a locomotive from Medicine Hat to nearby Dunmore. The route would take them along a winding stretch of track that follows a coulee (a deep ravine). There, they were to switch engines and crews with the Spokane Flyer.

The trip was a smooth one until suddenly a headlight appeared from around a curve in the track. The brightness blinded Twohey. They were on a collision course with an oncoming train.

"Jump!" Twohey yelled, but there was no time. The engineer and the stoker stood paralyzed with fear as the speeding train hurtling toward them sounded a warning blast from its whistle. Then, in eerie silence, the other train veered ever so slightly, and the two trains passed one another. In keeping with railroad tradition, passengers and crew waved toward Day and Twohey who stared in disbelief. The other train was travelling along nonexistent tracks, its huge iron wheels running smoothly, silently—and impossibly—just above the ground. Then, as quickly as it had appeared, the approaching train vanished.

Badly shaken, the two men looked at one another and shook their heads. It was their tacit agreement that neither of them was willing to acknowledge what had just happened.

A few days later, Day and Twohey chanced to see each other as they were out walking near downtown Medicine Hat. Twohey confessed that he hadn't been able to shake the strange incident of the phantom train. He was so troubled by it that he had even gone to see a fortune teller. She assured him that he was in perfect health, before adding the dreadful news that he would be dead within a month. Twohey told his workmate that, for safety's sake, he had arranged to work in the rail yards rather than on the trains for the rest of the month. Day understood completely. The two shook hands and parted.

An engineer named James Nicholson took Twohey's next shift on the train with Day. Their assignment was the same: they were to meet the Spokane Flyer at Dunmore in order to exchange locomotives and crews. All went well until they reached the bend on the tracks where the phantom train had appeared. Day's blood must have run cold when he heard that same warning whistle getting louder and louder. He knew exactly what was coming. Nicholson, however, was taken by complete surprise as the headlight from the oncoming train streaked across his line of vision. Seconds later, the phantom train, with its ghostly occupants waving, passed alongside Day and Nicholson and then vanished before their eyes.

What was happening? By now three responsible railroad employees had seen the same paranormal phenomenon. Was this a mass hallucination or a waking nightmare of some sort? Whatever it was, all three men were terrified.

A few days later, still struggling to act as though nothing out of the ordinary had happened, Day turned up for work and was relieved to learn that he had been assigned to yard duty. A man named Harry Thompson would take his place as firefighter on the eastbound run with James Nicholson.

As Thompson and Nicholson's train sped east they saw another train travelling toward them. Nicholson, who had seen the phantom train once, decided to ignore the mirage, but Thompson did not have that confidence. Seconds before a grinding head-on collision, Thompson jumped clear of the coal car where he had been working. The move saved his life. The oncoming train was not a phantom, and Thompson was the only member of either crew to survive the crash. It was passenger train 514 out of Lethbridge on a scheduled run to Medicine Hat. Bob Twohey was the engineer. He and seven passengers were killed that day, as was Nicholson in the eastbound locomotive. What a tragedy that the phantom sightings had not been understood. Both engineers had seen the phantom train, a supernatural forerunner of what was to come.

Pub Crawl

The old pubs that dot England's landscape all seem to have at least one ghost story to tell, but haunted pubs in Canada are a bit more unusual. The Cat 'n' Fiddle Pub in Calgary, Alberta, however, could give most of those British watering holes a run for their money. And this place comes by its ghosts honestly because the old building housed a funeral home until 1992.

The first encounter one of the owners had with any of the "spirits" in her bar wasn't frightening at all. She explains that she was only puzzled when she saw a cloud of "grey mist" form just above the floor. She sensed that the vaporous figure was female and that it meant her no harm.

Her second experience, however, was considerably less pleasant. The personable woman was working at her desk in the pub's basement, the area that was previously reserved for embalming and cremation. As the owner worked away, she suddenly sensed that someone was standing behind her. She looked around to see who had come downstairs, but there was no one in the room with her. She turned back and saw a shadow falling across her computer screen. Too frightened to move, she sat staring at the screen while her body became colder and colder. Chilled to the bone, she watched the shadow move until it brushed up against her before finally disappearing. Not surprisingly, the woman felt cold for the next two days.

She is certainly not the only person working at the pub who is aware of the ghosts. One particular cook prided himself on being a skeptic—until a pair of women's red shoes and the hem of a red dress materialized before his eyes and then disappeared again. Staff members know when the lady in red is present because she brings a lavender scent with her.

Because hauntings are so closely correlated with electrical or electronic devices, it's no surprise that the television at the bar can be troublesome. Sometime the on/off button refuses to work. Other times the sound on the television will go from muted to blaring, all while no one's been near the set. The haunted hijinks are especially annoying when the television is turned to a sports game that's at a critical juncture. All the patrons are tense, waiting for the next play—then it simply changes to another channel. People try to blame one another for this when, in fact, no one has been near the television—no human that is.

One morning, footsteps echoed through the building, and the staff feared there was an intruder. They searched the place from basement to roof, but they couldn't find anyone. Another time there was a break-in at the pub. The burglar was trying to get away with as much as he could as quickly as he could, but he dropped everything and ran after glancing in the mirror and seeing that something was standing right behind him—something that could only be seen in the mirror.

Interestingly, the men's washroom, which was an addition to the original building, also has a ghost. Its resident apparition wears tails and a top hat and has been seen moving across the floor before vanishing into a solid wall.

Even the street outside the pub is thought to be haunted. On frigid, snowy winter nights, people have heard the sound of a motorcycle racing along. Of course no one would be riding a motorcycle under those conditions, so it's thought that some biker is eternally enjoying his last ride. Perhaps his funeral was once held at the old funeral home where the pub now welcomes guests.

And so life goes on at this haunted pub, as does the afterlife. Next time you go out for a quick bite to eat, perhaps down to your neighbourhood pub, hoist a brew to those who have gone before and whose souls may remain.

Pumphouse Phantoms

Considering the history of the Pumphouse Theatre in Calgary, Alberta, it's not surprising that it's haunted. The building dates back to 1913 when it served as Pumphouse #2 and drew water from the Bow River. The building became redundant during the mid-1920s, but it was left standing.

During the Great Depression, the old pumphouse building became a temporary and unofficial shelter for unemployed men, known as hoboes, who were making their way across Canada. Tales from that era often glorify the hoboes, but in reality these people had little—including little respect for life. Their justice system was swift and permanent. As a result, there is no question that murders were committed in the otherwise unused building, and it's generally agreed that the ghosts hail from that era.

In the late 1960s, the building was finally scheduled for demolition. Fortunately, drama teacher and advocate Joyce Doolittle had a better idea. She spearheaded a complete renovation, and in 1972 the dilapidated old building was reborn as an impressive theatre complex.

Bob Eberle who managed the facility in the late 1970s declared, "We may have a new theatre but the ghosts of the past still haunt us." Truer words were apparently never spoken.

Leslie Holth, who was once general manager of the theatre, recalls an incident at the beginning of a particular performance. The director had indicated that the auditorium should be dark and silent for a few seconds. Unfortunately, just at that moment, music reverberated throughout the hall spoiling the intended effect. At intermission, the director approached the operators in the control booth to ask why they had played music when he'd asked for silence. The stage manager and the sound operator were both as puzzled as the director; they certainly hadn't created the interruption.

Fittingly, one of the stages at the Pumphouse is named after Joyce Doolittle. According to the theatre's website, the wife of an employee was once in "the Joyce Doolittle Theatre lobby and heard what sounded like a music box playing in the corner. She called her husband and asked if any music was being played in the dressing room or the theatre. He told her 'no' and inquired as to why she would ask." When his wife told him what she had heard the man was stunned. The woman would have had no idea that the area where she heard the music had once contained a player piano.

As is often the case with a haunted building, employees and volunteers occasionally report walking through pockets of inexplicably cold air or hearing the sounds of footsteps or laughter coming from an area they know is empty. Many people associated with the Pumphouse dismiss the ghost stories, but others like to pay their respects and greet the spirits as they enter the haunted building. Leslie Holth stands firmly in that camp: "They say we should befriend that which we don't know and thereby will come to appreciate a greater understanding of our world."

No wonder those souls that remain in the Pumphouse feel welcome to haunt the theatre.

Educated Entities

A rundown old house once stood near the University of Alberta campus in Edmonton, Alberta. The house should have been demolished sooner than it was, but the place was still a profitable investment for its owner as well as a convenient temporary home for students. And it was haunted—by spine-chilling voices from its past.

A student who lived in the house explained to a reporter with the *Edmonton Journal* that she and her housemates would regularly hear the sounds of a man's angry voice followed by a woman's pleading voice and a child's plaintive cries. An archival search confirmed that the house had been the site of a double homicide and suicide in the 1930s. The horror of that terrible tragedy apparently still echoed inside the walls.

There are also several haunted buildings on the campus itself. Corbett Hall, one of the oldest University of Alberta buildings, is home to a benign presence known as Emily. Her haunting has become so integral to the school's popular history that she is occasionally acknowledged in alumni magazines. Emily is only ever seen walking across the stage in Corbett Hall, so witnesses have speculated that her image is eternally reliving the happy moment of her graduation ceremony. She doesn't seem to be aware of today's world, which is a shame considering she's so fondly regarded.

An old house on the campus ring road was the home of Dr. and Mrs. Robert Newton while he was president of the university in the 1940s. Many people believe that Mrs. Newton's spirit has never left the place. Small objects frequently go missing only to turn up later in a completely illogical place, and her spirit is also said to turn lights on and off.

One winter evening, a group of people all felt a gust of wind come up the stairs while they worked away on the second floor of the Newtons' former home. They all agreed that someone must have opened and closed the front door. This was a bit concerning because they knew they had locked themselves in. No one wanted to go downstairs alone to investigate, so they all went together. They found the door locked, just as it should have been, and that there was no sign it had been opened. Feeling somewhat emboldened, they set about searching the house but didn't find anything out of the ordinary.

Not surprisingly, most people decided to leave after that unnerving interruption. Only the instructor and one student stayed behind. All was quiet in the house until they both heard the sound of a heavy roll of paper being laid out. That was enough for them. They too left the building, thinking that if Mrs. Newton wanted to wallpaper her house then they would just leave her to it.

The Housing Union Building (HUB) is an important part of campus life and consists of residences, retail shops, and places to relax or study. Before this unique building could be constructed, a number of houses that had stood on the site for many decades had to be demolished. Interestingly, at least one of those houses was haunted. People walking through HUB will occasionally notice a pillar of cold air running through one part of the building—exactly where a haunted house once stood.

The University of Alberta has a beautiful old pump organ in Convocation Hall in the Old Arts Building. Legend has it that on the evening of November 11, 1939, and all during World War II, the instrument played "Taps" even though no one was ever seen near the organ.

Not to be outdone, the University of Calgary has at least one haunted building, according to an article in the *Calgary Herald*. The Earth Sciences Building is said to be the haunt of Mrs. Fish, the former dean of women students. Mrs. Fish served the university during the 1950s, when that campus was a satellite campus of the University of Alberta in Edmonton. Since her premature death, her likeness has been seen and recognized. She is thought to still be living her life, apparently unaware that it is now her afterlife. She haunts the place with phantom sounds and by opening and closing doors when there is no one near them—no one visible.

Welcome to the haunted halls of learning!

Living Ghost

When is a ghost story not a ghost story? Perhaps when an apparition is still alive. There aren't many true ghost stories that fit that category, but such events have been recorded. In Lethbridge, Alberta, for instance, the disembodied cries of a little girl have been heard echoing through the Bowman Arts Centre. After some research, employees of the centre discovered a little Chinese girl wearing traditional trousers was once mistaken for a boy and punished for going to the girls' washroom at the centre. The child's trauma still echoed through the building even though the child, now an adult and living in another province, was very much alive.

BRITISH COLUMBIA

Haunted Hospital

As spooky as a late-night stroll through a cemetery may be, graveyards rarely seem to be haunted. It's hospitals that you should stay away from if you're afraid of encountering a ghost. Many hospitals across the country are haunted, and the old burn unit at Vancouver General Hospital in Vancouver, British Columbia, was no exception. The resident ghost was thought to be the spirit of an especially popular patient. By now, there is some controversy as to whether the man's name was Jim or Douglas, but there has never been any debate about the last weeks of his life and how hard he struggled to survive the terrible burns he suffered when a grain elevator caught fire.

At the hospital, the man was placed alone in a room in order to reduce his risk of infection. Other than the attentive medical staff that came and went, the patient was by himself in that room for weeks enduring virtually unbearable pain. His only diversion was listening to a small bedside radio. He became a favourite of the hospital staff because, despite his injuries, his mood was always positive. Clearly he had made up his mind to get his life back. In the end though, his body defeated his mind. Despite everyone's best efforts, he finally succumbed to his massive burns.

It wasn't long before another burn victim occupied the well-liked man's former hospital room, and that was when members of the nursing staff began to feel an invisible presence in that room. The sensation was so intense that, when one nurse went into the room to change a patient's dressings, she was sure that her colleague had followed her in and was standing right behind her. Firm in that knowledge, she reached back and handed the other nurse a tray of bandages. The metal tray clattered to the floor because her co-worker wasn't there. She and the patient were the only living beings in that small room.

Another nurse had an even eerier encounter. One day, when that same room was empty, she heard the sounds of laboured breathing coming from the freshly made bed. Then, as she stared in disbelief, the sheets on the bed began to wrinkle and bunch up as though a patient she could not see was trying, in vain, to get comfortable.

People have also reported inexplicable shapes undulating through that room when it was apparently empty.

Once, a very sick woman who was staying in a nearby room asked if the kind young man who had sat with her during the long night would be back to comfort her the next night. The staff was shocked because they had checked on her frequently through the night and she was alone. When the patient described her nocturnal visitor, she described that brave burn victim who had lost his fight for life.

On another occasion, a burn patient enthusiastically described a young man who had come to his bedside and had made several helpful suggestions about how best to cope with his pain. Again, the patient offered a detailed description of the burn victim. The staff knew immediately that their deceased patient was helping them to help others.

There were other signs of a supernatural presence, which is not surprising for such a haunted area. Sudden cold gusts of air blew through the room when there was no physical reason for a draft. The washroom taps would turn on and off when no one was near them, and the toilet would flush randomly even when the bathroom was empty.

Periodically, different members of the hospital staff reported hearing the sound of the victim's bedside radio playing in that room—the radio that had helped the young man cope with the last few days of his life.

The burn unit has been moved now, and it seems that the popular young patient who lost his life has moved on to his afterlife. Rest in peace, young man.

The Headless Brakeman

Hub Clark was a railway brakeman. On a particularly cold and rainy night, Hub was assigned to inspect the rails on Granville Street rail yard in downtown Vancouver, British Columbia. Dressed in traditional black and white striped overalls, Hub walked along on the wet, slippery gravel beside the tracks, carrying a lantern to light his way. All was well until the poor man lost his footing and fell. Tragically, he hit his head on the track and knocked himself out. Moments later, a passenger train came barreling down the track and ran over poor Hub, decapitating him instantly.

Since then, there have been sightings of a strange light swaying back and forth on cold rainy nights, as if someone is holding a lantern while walking along those tracks. A few brave and curious folks have dared to linger, watching the strange glow as it approaches. Their patience and courage have been rewarded by a fleeting glimpse of a headless man wearing black and white striped overalls.

Perhaps poor Hub is looking for his head—or doing his job into eternity, warning people away from the treacherous wet gravel near the tracks.

Spirits with Your Meal

Gastown in downtown Vancouver, British Columbia, is said to be the most haunted neighbourhood in the city, and the delightfully decorated Old Spaghetti Factory does its part to hold up that reputation.

The building itself has had a long and colourful history; it was a grocer's, a train station, and a factory. Then, during its conversion to a restaurant, the new owners bought an old trolley bus to use as a unique seating area. Many other old objects have since been brought in to add interest to the décor. All of these factors are an invitation to a haunting. Apparently, the invitation was accepted.

Four ghosts have been identified. None of them seem to have any connection to, or even any awareness of, the others. The Little Red Man is the most troublesome spirit in the place. He's also extremely easily identified because, as his name suggests, he's not very tall and he's seen wearing a red shirt and red long johns. He's clearly aware of the people working around him because he often calls them by name.

One of Little Red Man's favourite haunts is the women's washroom, where he seems to thoroughly enjoy startling patrons before disappearing from sight. One woman was especially quick with her phone and took a picture of the strange apparition. When she got back to her table and looked at her screen, there was a swirling black cloud where the apparition had been.

The most troublesome ghost is that of a little boy who appears very real. With his old-fashioned clothing, however, he is decidedly out of place. Like Little Red Man, this childish entity seems aware of his surroundings and even calls some staff members by their names. A psychic who visited the restaurant believed that, in life, the entity's name was Edward. He's a mischievous wraith who sometimes interferes with the staff's work. After the restaurant closes at night, the staff takes time to set up the tables for the next day's lunch rush. Apparently this routine doesn't please the mischievous wraith because he's been known to bend the cutlery that has just been set out on the tables.

The boy's image is so lifelike that a server once chased him to the restaurant door where she confronted him. Just after his lifeless eyes met her gaze, the young woman ran to the manager and quit on the spot. Another server, this one with nerves of steel, actually pursued the ghostly urchin and, when she caught up to him, asked him what he wanted. The ghost replied, "Put on some music so the other ghosts will come out." As soon as he spoke, the apparition disappeared.

Perhaps one of the other ghosts that the little spectre had in mind was the phantom of a little girl. The child's revenant sits quietly holding the string of a balloon. When a server asked her why she was sitting there, she answered quietly that she was waiting for her mother.

When a group of students tried to make a film about the ghosts in the Old Spaghetti Factory, they asked for the ghosts' co-operation. Their request was met with a series of loud sounds and a severe drop in the room's temperature. That one time, at least, the spirits were accommodating.

The trolley car, old number fifty-three, is home to the ghost of a trolley conductor in a full old-fashioned uniform. Years ago, a quick-thinking witness took the ghost's photograph, and a framed enlargement of that print hangs proudly on the restaurant's wall.

The spirit is thought to be that of a conductor who died in an accident close to nearby Waterfront Station, which has been called "the most haunted building in Vancouver."

Waterfront Station is an impressive old building dating back to 1914, when travelling by train was considered the height of elegance. In addition to its use as a train station, the enormous building also housed fancy restaurants, a dance hall, and prestigious offices. And, it would seem, virtually all those areas are haunted.

A trio of apparitions is often seen there late at night. The spectres are completely benign and merely sit quietly together on a bench, as if they are waiting for their train to arrive.

One night, a security guard working the graveyard shift thought he heard music coming from somewhere in the building. He followed the sound to the station's former dance hall, where the distinctive strains of a 1920s tune echoed throughout the room. The man scanned the room in disbelief until he spotted a vague figure off in a corner. It was the image of a woman, dressed in period clothes and dancing a solitary waltz. He summoned his courage and took a step into the room intending to approach her, but as he did, the music stopped and the vision of the woman disappeared.

She may have been the ghost that another guard saw when he walked into a storage room. That apparition held out her hand to the man, but he didn't accept her overture. Instead he ran down the hall as quickly as he could.

One of those storage rooms was the setting for a truly bizarre sight, even by supernatural standards. A man once made his way into a room full of old desks. When he reached the far wall of the room, several of the desks lifted up and moved around. Some piled themselves on top of one another, but the worst one—from the witness's point of view—was the one that blocked the doorway. With adrenaline surging, the trapped man made his way to the door, shoved the desk out of his way, and ran along the hall and down the stairs as fast as he could. In his haste, he probably didn't hear the phantom footfalls that are often heard in that corridor and stairwell.

A few years ago, two office workers were chatting in the station when a woman joined them. Neither of them recognized her, so they finished their conversation and then turned toward the stranger. They both described her as being attractive, with long auburn hair, and wearing a fancy blue blouse that was decidedly out of fashion.

The image met each of their gazes before telling them, "I'll come back another time." With that, the pretty woman vanished.

It seems the ghosts at Waterfront Station have earned the building its reputation as the most haunted in Vancouver.

The *Eliza Anderson*

When she was new, the *Eliza Anderson* was as fine a ship as you could find on the West Coast. But by 1897, the side-wheeler had served the Olympia, Washington-to-Victoria, British Columbia, mail run for nearly forty years, and she was effectively worn out. Her owner, the Northwestern Steamship Company, floated the ageing craft to a holding dock until it could arrange to tow her to the scrapyard. The company must not have needed the money it would recover from salvaging the *Eliza Anderson*; the abandoned ship was left to rot in a muddy, weed-infested slough. Over the next two years, the vessel sat there deteriorating due to natural causes, a process that was hurried along by the vandals and scavengers who stripped many parts from the once-proud craft.

In August of 1899, the *Eliza Anderson* was brought out of retirement for one last voyage—a voyage to a paranormal encounter. Her crew for this trip from Victoria to Alaska via the Inside Passage was a mismatched bunch of sailors chosen in great haste and led by a captain named Tom Powers. Potential profit was the only motive for this reclamation, and so only minimal repair work was done to make the neglected and abused ship seaworthy once more.

In order to make the venture more financially rewarding, the ship's owners not only took freight but passengers too. Most of them were prospectors, fortune hunters much more interested in finding the gold mother lode than in getting along with their fellow passengers. The *Eliza Anderson* was not long out of port when serious squabbles began on board. The crew members were fighting among themselves, as were the passengers. Before long, animosity developed between the two groups as well. This trip was not destined to be pleasant.

Not long after this vessel of discontent passed the port of Prince Rupert, British Columbia, en route to Alaska, she ran into a heavy storm. Tempers on board flared even more. It was not until the chief engineer came topside and reported that coal supplies were dangerously low that all of those on board the *Eliza Anderson* realized this was no time for petty quarrels. If they didn't work together to get this ship of fools safely through the storm, none of them would live to tell of it.

Captain Powers immediately ordered passengers and crew alike to begin breaking apart anything on board that was flammable and not structurally necessary. If they didn't have coal, then they'd use whatever they could to generate enough steam to get them through the gale. Once a supply of flammable material was stockpiled, the majority of the badly frightened men resorted to the only other helpful activity they could think of: prayer.

It would take divine intervention, they were sure, to keep this badly neglected, forty-year-old piece of scrap metal from sinking. She was being buffeted badly enough by the high waves to frighten everyone on board. When the force of the storm toppled the smoke-stack and sent it crashing onto the deck, all on board knew that the storm was stronger than their ship. Those who'd been to sea before knew that such an imbalance was a recipe for disaster.

Captain Powers recruited every person in his care to work toward getting the ship through the storm. He ordered some to clean the steam pumps, some to dump oil from their cargo hold into the waves with the hope of calming them, and others to work with the rudder. Those not otherwise occupied broke up more wood to stoke the fire.

Despite everyone's efforts, the best the *Eliza Anderson* could manage was to survive as the storm raged around her. The crew had no hope of generating enough power to move away from the foul weather. All they could do was pray they would still be floating by the time the storm had either dissipated or moved on. After two days and two nights of constantly battling the elements, all on board were exhausted. The storm raged around them. No relief appeared to be in sight. The end, in the form of certain death for all, seemed imminent.

By the third morning, Captain Powers had lost his bearings. He had no idea which direction was where. The situation was utterly hopeless. There was no way of knowing whether they were going to be buffeted against rocks, or how much more of a beating the ship's structure would take from the winds and the waves before she started to crack. Powers knew that if either of those possibilities occurred, it would only be a matter of time before crew and passengers alike were all tossed to a watery grave.

Just as their fate seemed inevitable, a sailor on the bridge thought he spotted something through the curtain of torrential rain. He hesitated before announcing his sighting, for he couldn't believe what he was seeing. There appeared to be a small boat approaching on the waves. As it came closer and closer, the sailor was able to make out an outline, the outline of a lone occupant in a woefully inadequate craft rowing with all his might toward the *Eliza Anderson*. He tied his rowboat to the larger ship's ropes and seconds later, "a veritable giant of a man, raw-boned and muscular," was on board the distressed ship.

Captain Powers, his crew, and the passengers watched in disbelief as this larger-than-life figure took the wheel of their ravaged vessel. Almost imperceptibly at first, and then more obviously, the seemingly doomed ship began moving in a specific direction. No longer was she just being tossed about at the whim of the angry wind. Within hours, they'd navigated to the edge of the storm. The seas calmed, and the danger lessened. Several hours later, land was in sight. The terrified souls on board the *Eliza Anderson* were no longer in peril.

As silently as he had boarded the ship, the mysterious stranger left. He made his way down a rope ladder to his little craft, untied it, and rowed away. The thoughts of those left behind on the *Eliza Anderson* immediately turned from the presence that had steered them to safety, to the task of finding help in this isolated location. And, once they did, it was some time before anyone was ready to discuss the unexpected rescue. By then, many of the people who had been on the ship had decided that the phantom who'd piloted them to safety had only been a figment of their collective imaginations.

In 1899, an anonymous writer who had been on board the *Eliza Anderson* and witnessed the supernatural rescue submitted an article to a newspaper in Seattle, Washington. He maintained that he had recognized the saviour as the ghost of Captain Tom Wright, who had owned and operated the *Eliza Anderson* until his death. He wrote, "Captain Tom's spirit saw our danger. He knew and loved the *Anderson*, and that was how it happened that a stranger came out of the storm and brought us safely to land."

We can never know for sure what happened that stormy, fateful day off the coast of British Columbia, but it would certainly seem as though supernatural intervention played an important lifesaving role. We do know that all on board escaped with their lives, and that the *Eliza Anderson* never sailed again.

Haunting at the Heriot Bay Inn

The history of the Heriot Bay Inn on Quadra Island, British Columbia, is long, colourful, and haunted. Lois Taylor, part owner of the inn, has been associated with the old building for forty-five years and seems as dedicated and fond of the resident ghosts as she is of the inn itself.

One ghost is the spirit of a woman who, for the most part, is a passive gentle soul. She has, however, been heard moving furniture around on the second floor when there was no one on that level—no one alive, anyway. Lois and her colleagues learned a bit more about the ghost when a man visiting from California asked to see some of the rooms. The front desk staff handed him some room keys so that he could choose the one that would suit him best.

When the visitor came back downstairs, he explained that he was psychic and there was a spirit of a woman in a room who communicated to him that she did not like men in her room. She wasn't threatening to him at all. When he asked why she was there, she explained simply that she was waiting. It's likely that she is the same entity who's been seen in the lounge knitting. She is also frequently seen looking out of second-storey windows.

One day a woman came hurrying into the inn saying that she'd seen a woman at an upstairs window who seemed to be in great distress. The staff accompanied the concerned person upstairs, where they found the room completely empty.

And then there is the ghost of the man. He is not as content as the female phantom. Lois describes him as "gruff" and "not as happy." This haunting dates back to the early days of the last century. The man may have been a logger or perhaps a fisherman. Some say he was murdered, while others say he was the murderer. No matter what the manner of his death, his body is buried on a lot adjacent to the inn, and his spirit is frequently in and around the inn. Housekeepers making their rounds have felt his negative energy and have simply learned to work around it.

Writer and photographer Tanya Storr has great affection for Quadra Island and especially the compelling ghost stories associated with the Heriot Bay Inn. "Many former rationalists who say they never used to believe in the supernatural have changed their tune after encounters with uncanny phenomena at the inn," she wrote. What follows are first-hand accounts from Tanya's files of what three people experienced at the Heriot Bay Inn.

A bartender who had worked at the Heriot Bay Inn for many years had an eerie encounter in the pub one beautiful autumn day in 1987. The weather was far too nice for anyone to want to be inside, and so there were no customers at the bar. The bartender was taking advantage of the lull by catching up on chores. She was standing on a stool stocking the beer fridge with her back to the front door when she heard the door open and close. Then she felt a draft and, at the same time, felt as though someone was watching her. She didn't turn around right away because she didn't want to drop any of the bottles she was holding.

She knew, though, that a customer had come into the bar because she could hear the shuffling of his pants. She glanced toward the man to indicate that she would be right with him. The man had a beard and wore a dark canvas coat that was dripping wet, as if he'd just come inside to get out of a heavy rainstorm—even though it hadn't rained for days.

The bartender could see the man in her peripheral vision as she set down the last of the bottles she was carrying. A few seconds later she turned around, smiled, and started to ask, "Can I get you something to drink?"

But the words died on her lips. No one was there.

If the barmaid had been a skeptic before, then this incident changed her mind, even though it was the only encounter she ever had with the Heriot Bay Inn's resident ghost.

A former resident manager of the hotel will never forget an experience he had one cold winter night in the 1980s. He was alone in the hotel after the bar had closed when he heard a commotion outside. Thinking that stray dogs were getting into garbage containers, he went out to shoo the animals away. But once he was outside, all was quiet, and there was no movement on the property. When he turned to look back at the lodge, however, he had the shock of his life. The first floor of the hotel was ablaze with light. This couldn't be; he'd just left the building and knew that it should be dark.

He hurried back inside, only to find everything still locked. He walked through the building, thinking that someone must have broken in, but there was nothing at all to be seen, no animals, and certainly no people. In short there was nothing to explain the initial noises or the first-floor lights.

Demonstrating a gift for the understatement, the man concluded, "The whole thing was pretty spooky."

During another winter, a local man rented a room at the Heriot Bay Inn for one month. As this was the off-season, and he was the only guest, he had the perfect opportunity to encounter some of the hotel's more ethereal attractions.

He described being upstairs in his room, alone in the empty hotel. As he lay on his bed, he could hear footsteps walking along the corridor. At first he presumed that another guest had checked in. He waited to hear another room door open, but that never happened.

Evening after evening, he heard the same footsteps; the recurrence began to frustrate the man. Occasionally he would get up, open his door, and look out into the hallway, but it was always empty—as far as he could see anyway. He told himself that the noises he'd heard were simply the sounds that old buildings make, but he never had much luck convincing himself. In his mind, he was positive that he had heard a person walking along the corridor.

One night, the hotel manager invited his long-term guest and another man to his apartment in the hotel. The trio was enjoying watching movies on television, secure in the knowledge that they were locked into an otherwise empty building.

But they soon heard footsteps along the hall. This time the distinctive sounds went down the stairs and into the pub. The three men looked at one another in confusion. Worried that someone had broken in, all three of them ran to the main floor, determined to catch the intruder. But the area was empty, and all the doors were still locked. They agreed to split up. One man searched through the tackle shop, another the kitchen, and the third searched the pub. They could not find anyone. They even searched under pool tables, in washrooms, and anywhere they could think to look. They concluded, ironically, "there wasn't a soul there."

That should have been a relief to the three men, but sadly it wasn't because they were certain that they had heard someone walking through the building.

Another eerie encounter occurred while Lois was singing during an open mic session and her daughter was serving drinks. From the stage, Lois could see that her daughter was standing stock-still and staring at the floor. As soon as Lois finished her song, she went over to see what the trouble was. The front of a bottle of amaretto that had been standing on a nearby shelf had blown out; the liqueur was dripping out and making a sticky puddle on the floor. No one had been near the bottle at the time.

The good-natured group that had gathered decided that the ghost of the woman was feeling thirsty that night. The house bought a round of the liqueur for everyone there, and together they raised their glasses to offer "a toast to the ghost."

Mandy

Quesnel, British Columbia, lies roughly halfway between Prince George and Williams Lake. Perhaps because of its relative isolation, the small city has always had a strong sense of community. The local museum, for instance, proudly displays stories and objects from the area's past. One of those objects is an antique doll called Mandy, which came to the museum after a woman named Lisa found it in an old trunk tucked away in her grandmother's basement. It was immediately clear that this was no ordinary doll. For one thing, the doll was very old and singularly unattractive, with a cracked porcelain face, a ripped cloth body, and ragged, dirty clothes.

Even so, Lisa thought that she would keep Mandy as a memento. And she did, until a series of unexplained and disturbing events changed the young woman's mind. The first oddity Lisa noticed was at night. She would hear a baby crying even though there was no baby anywhere near. Inexplicable breezes blowing inside the house accompanied those phantom cries. When Lisa heard a window slam closed and found the spike that was supposed to hold it open lying on the floor, she decided that Mandy would have to go. She donated the toy to the museum.

That was in 1991. Since then, Mandy has drawn a host of visitors and has earned quite a reputation for herself. Some folks are sure the doll is possessed although no one is sure by what. Mandy has been held responsible for many eerie occurrences.

Artefacts acquired by the Quesnel and District Museum must be catalogued and photographed. While an experienced museum photographer was taking shots of the newly acquired doll, she and the friend who was with her during the shoot both felt extremely uncomfortable.

In order to get the job done—at least to the point where the film had been developed to produce negatives—the pair tried to ignore their feelings of discomfort. As soon as the negatives were hung to dry, they immediately tidied up, locked the museum, and left for the day. The next day the museum's curator described the mess in the developing room as looking like "a small child had had a temper tantrum."

Ross Mitchell, a photographer with the *Quesnel Cariboo Observer* also had an interesting experience with the photos that he took at the museum. Although he took pictures of many exhibits, the bulk of the pictures he took were of Mandy. When Mitchell returned to his office and tried to print off contact sheets of the photographs, the paper did not emerge from the developer. The potential pictures simply vanished somewhere inside the machine. While he was attempting to solve this problem, he heard footsteps in the office area above the developing room. Thinking there must be intruders in the building because he was supposed to be alone, he went up to check, but he could find no source for the sounds.

Seth Gotro, a photographer with the local paper also had a bizarre experience trying to take Mandy's picture. He reported that the doll seemed to "turn her head away from the lens so that I might not get her on film." Determined to complete the shoot nevertheless, he took the doll out of its glass case "and sat her on a bed. She seemed to be grinning at me as the flash hit her face."

A visitor to the museum from Calgary, Alberta, tried to videotape the slightly smiling doll. As she was filming, the woman remembered thinking that the doll did not like having her picture taken. She did not have time to dwell on this rather odd thought, however, because an indicator light on the video recorder began to flash intermittently. When she moved along to the next exhibit, the camera worked properly again.

Mandy apparently wasn't content with disrupting the woman's filming though. When the visitor got home and tried to play the videotape, it became wedged in her VCR and could only be removed forcibly. She never did get to view the tape.

Perhaps one day Mandy will share her secrets with the living. Until then, those who believe this intriguing artefact hosts a presence will have to be content to speculate.

In a related story, Lizzie who "lived" at the Museum of the Paranormal in Niagara-on-the-Lake, Ontario, came close to giving Mandy a run for her money in the creepy category. She was displayed in a dark corner of the museum's attic, propped up on a doll-sized rocking chair. Some people have gone so far as to say that Lizzie was "full of dark energy." The doll's eyes would follow visitors, and she was even known to wink at them. The Museum of the Paranormal has closed its doors for the last time, which certainly begs the question: Where have Lizzie and all the other creepy artefacts taken their supernatural energy now?

Negative Imprint

Back in 1975, a horrifying story was making the rounds about a strange sight at the top of the hill in Beacon Hill Park in Victoria, British Columbia. People were seeing a young woman with a dark tan, long and blonde hair wearing white slacks standing at the top of the hill.

Witnesses said her face was contorted in a silent scream and her arms outstretched in an apparent plea for help. The manifestation exuded such terror that no one wanted to approach her, but a few brave ones tried to help. Unfortunately, by the time they'd climbed the hill, the vision had vanished. Talk turned to the possibility of a ghost haunting Beacon Hill, but that wasn't really the case. The girl wasn't dead—at least not yet.

After a time, the disturbing image faded, as did all the interest in the bizarre apparition.

It wasn't until the autumn of 1983 that the mystery of this bizarre sighting was solved. A girl's body was found hidden in undergrowth at the base of the hill. She had long dark hair and was wearing dark blue jeans. The discovery was a tragic end to a search that had begun some weeks before, when the young woman had been reported missing. When police found the body it was determined the girl had been murdered.

Not long after that, some of the people who had witnessed the pathetic sight up on the hill eight years earlier realized that the victim's body resembled the image they had seen, but in reverse, as if the actual person was a negative of the apparition they had seen. Where the phantom had been wearing white slacks and had long blonde hair with tanned skin, the body was clothed in blue jeans, had long dark hair, and white skin. Somehow the victim's soul had acted as a forerunner for the girl's tragic death.

Robin Skelton and Jean Kozocari examine the mystery in *A Gathering of Ghosts* (1989).

The screaming ghost of Beacon Hill Park foretold the future. It is hard to determine, however, whether the young woman herself, by a kind of astral projection, was foreseeing her own death or whether, by a curious twist of time, the place pre-recorded a memory before the even had occurred.

The only certainty is this: since the murder of that unfortunate young woman, there have been no known sightings of that spectre in Beacon Hill Park.

Sagebrush Shades

Actors and the crews that support their theatrical efforts tend to be a dedicated and emotional group of individuals. An actor's job is an odd one at best: In a highly contrived setting, with the help of the crew, he or she works to convince another group of individuals, the audience, that something fictional is actually fact. Judging by the number of haunted theatres, this kind of situation is apparently a formula for phantoms.

They call him Albert. Albert the Apparition is the resident wraith at the Sagebrush Theatre in the city of Kamloops in south-central British Columbia. His presence has been well documented over the years.

The hauntings began in 1939, just after several graves in the Lorne Street Cemetery were excavated and the bodies moved to a location on Pleasant Street, near the Sagebrush Theatre. Many people believe that the spirit is the ghost of Albert Mallot, the first man ever to be hanged in Kamloops.

One of Albert's favourite haunts is along the catwalk, high above the stage. Theatre technicians, people who are trained to be both observant and analytical, have stared in amazement as a man dressed in old-fashioned clothes casually stands on the suspended platform. The first time Albert was spotted, the worker searched for what she presumed to be a trespasser. Although no one could have left that isolated area without her knowledge, she could not find the man. He had simply disappeared.

The next time Albert was seen in approximately the same part of the Sagebrush, the spectre did not wait to be hunted down. He vanished before the witness's eyes.

After the resident phantom was seen sitting in one of the audi-torium seats, employee Roger Lantz made a bold overture. He went into the seating area of the theatre and sat down in that very same spot. As soon as he was comfortably settled, Lantz challenged the ghost to do something about his live presence in the ghost's preferred chair. Perhaps Roger would not have been so daring if he had known that in life, Albert had a reputation for being mean at the best of times—he was executed committing murder in cold blood. Oddly, the ghost apparently backed down from Roger's challenge.

Judging from the ghostly occurrences during the show later

that night, death had only slightly improved Albert's disposition. No matter what Roger did, he could not get the sound system to cooperate. The levels would not stay set. Sometimes sound would come from the wrong speaker and sometimes not at all, with the unfortunate result that cues were missed throughout the entire production. By the end of that evening, Albert had made his point to the daring Roger Lantz, who will likely never challenge a ghost again. It seemed the ghost wasn't done, though, because Roger began experiencing oddities that no one else in the theatre ever encountered.

An "apport" is a small object that appears, apparently out of nowhere, in a place that is known to be haunted, and Roger suddenly became the recipient of many apports.

Roger explains, "What would happen is that I would hear a noise coming from the upstage left corner of the stage. The sound of something hitting the floor and rolling to a stop would get my attention every now and then. I would go looking, but I would find nothing. This went on for a while until one time I actually saw something fall. This time I went to investigate and found a pebble on the floor."

Roger didn't find the incident frightening, and that's a very good thing because there was more to come. "There was a period of time where this was almost a daily occurrence for me. I found it interesting that I was the only one who seemed to be around when it happened. I really began to look at the specific area where these pebbles came from. It was always right near the sink, [there was] usually about [a] 10-foot-square area where these pebbles would land."

This was puzzling to Roger because "There was nowhere that a pebble could come from. The ceiling above was a prefabricated con-crete floor piece that was completely smooth and free of any cracks or blemishes. I even went up in the lift to look closely at the ceiling. I found no source for a pebble to fall. For a time I had a collection of these pebbles on my fridge at home."

Then Albert upped his game. "Once a larger piece of concrete [approximately 5 centimetres across] hit the floor right beside me! Only in that case I had been talking about Albert during the day, and I may have even joked around about him. That particular event made the little hairs on my neck stand up. It was far away from the sink and it appeared it was meant for my head! That, as I recall, was the final time for that sort of event."

Roger continues, "I have often wondered what the significance of the pebbles was. I was usually alone in the building when this happened. If others were around I would show them the small pebble and they never heard or saw it fall. The most active time for this happening was from 1984 to 1987. I have been back there several times over the years and even stood there for a while to see if anything would happen. It never has since, at least to me."

Roger shares the commonly accepted theory of who the ghost was when he was alive, and why he's known as Albert. "I heard that a man named Albert was buried on the site where the theatre was built. Now there is a cemetery directly across the street. Were there some graves that may have been on the property where the theatre is built? That's certainly something to ponder. Whenever I go back to the Sagebrush I always 'talk' to Albert. I secretly hope that he is still around. Maybe next time I go there he will drop a pebble for me by the sink, just for old times' sake? I have rarely told this story to anyone, so maybe that will stir him again for me. He was always just a prankster in my mind, which I kind of appreciate."

Though Albert might have had an issue to settle with Roger, the phantom's instant dislike for another man, a stagehand, is more difficult to explain. In this case, Albert's motivation might have been obscure, but his sentiments were made very clear to the worker who was positioned on a platform high above the stage. As the worker concentrated on the job at hand, a bag of peanuts flew at him, narrowly missing his head. Not only was there no other human being in the area who might have propelled the missile, to do such a thing would have been a flagrant disregard for the well-known rules of theatre safety. No one associated with the theatre would ever have done anything so disrespectful or dangerous.

Conversely, Albert's spirit has also been credited with preventing what could have been a serious accident. A woman who was new to the job of operating the theatre's spotlights came into work early one evening. She was up on the catwalk rehearsing lighting changes when a voice chastised her for not wearing the requisite safety harness. Feeling embarrassed by her carelessness, she immediately fastened the belt around herself.

Seconds later, a light crashed down from above her. Had she not been tied in, the woman would doubtless have been hurt. Badly shaken, she made her way down to the stage, wanting to thank the person who had given her the timely warning. There was no one else anywhere in the theatre.

Some employees, uncomfortable with the feeling of being watched by invisible eyes, have actually resigned rather than risk any further supernatural encounters. And a cleaner, who initially announced that she was a skeptic by nature, fled the theatre after the cord of the vacuum cleaner she was using continually became unplugged and tied in knots.

By now, however, the ghost of Albert Mallot has earned an accepted place in the Kamloops theatre community.

Time Slips

Not all ghost stories involve the spirits of people. Places can also be haunted by the past, and witnesses claim that one of Victoria, British Columbia's major roads is just such a place. It's said that in the wee hours of the night during the month of October, modern Shelbourne Street harkens back to its past.

Folks who have seen this spooky transformation are usually driving south and are usually alone in their car. As their familiar surroundings change, they wonder if they've taken a wrong turn. But how could that be? They haven't turned at all. Worse, this is a route they know well. They know that there should be a paved road, lined with buildings and well-lit by streetlights. Instead they're looking at a rural scene: a country road with unkempt ditches at the sides and not a building in sight.

Taken aback by this strange sight, the lone driver inevitably wants to get his or her car turned around as quickly as possible, but the road is so narrow that it's impossible to make a U-turn without ending up in the ditch.

Just then, the scene shifts again and reverts to the modern well-lit paved road and contemporary buildings. The relief must be palpable, but there's still that nagging question: What just happened? Did the person see the ghost of what Shelbourne Street once was or momentarily travel back to that time? If that is the case, then the bizarre circumstances are an excellent example of a phenomenon known as retrocognition.

Another example was reported on a residential street in Metchosin, not far from Victoria, where people have watched in awe as a large red wagon filled with oak barrels is pulled along by two handsome draft horses. Some who have witnessed the supernatural event say that, after the anomaly passes, it morphs into a red delivery truck.

Yet another incidence of retrocognition took place in the province during the early 1930s at a party in a recently renovated house in Vancouver's West End. What makes this case even more intriguing is that a room full of people shared the encounter.

The story really starts in the early days of the last century, when a couple purchased a small parcel of land in what is now the West End of Vancouver. They built a home there and settled in. Neighbours later reported that the newcomers were rather an odd pair; the woman was extremely outgoing, but the man was a virtual recluse. No one in the area had a chance to learn much more than that because the woman died just six months later. The bereaved husband hastily sold the place and moved away.

No more is known about the house between that time and 1931, when a young couple purchased the place. Initially the two were delighted with their real estate investment and did not plan to make any changes to the interior layout. The master bedroom was on the main floor, which they felt was convenient.

But they felt uneasy right from their first night in that room. When that uncomfortable feeling didn't fade, the pair decided that some renovations would be necessary after all. They decided to sleep in another bedroom and to enlarge the living room to include most of what had been the original master bedroom.

It was not long before the changes were completed. The couple was so pleased with the way their home looked that they decided to invite their friends over for a housewarming party. The celebration started off wonderfully well. The guests seemed to be enjoying themselves in the newly enlarged living room. Then, according to a woman who had been a guest that evening, at "precisely eleven o'clock, the room became unaccountably cold." What happened next was far more concerning: "A whirlwind of nothingness" suddenly manifested in the part of the room that had been the master bedroom.

"Then, out of the whirlwind slowly emerged a massive four-poster bed on which a woman was lying, clearly at the point of departure from this life. Her eyes were fixed in fear and horror. Beside her was the indistinct figure of a man sitting in a Victorian chair at her bedside," the anonymous witness attested.

One of the other guests, a neighbour who had lived in the area a long time, shouted out that he recognized the apparitions. He identified them as the couple that had built the place.

The images didn't stay long, but they did succeed in bringing the party to an abrupt and early end. Agreeing not to tell anyone of the supernatural event they had just witnessed, the guests quickly dispersed.

Despite all the effort the new owners had put into the house, they realized they could never be comfortable staying there and immediately listed their home for sale. The couple was relieved the place sold quickly and, as they wanted to be clear of anything associated with the place, they arranged to sell all their newly purchased furniture, draperies, and even rugs.

The woman who provided the account of the party, including the manifestation of the bed and the apparitions, went to the auction of her friends' belongings. Perhaps she was interested in purchasing some of the items herself, for she inspected the articles carefully. The living room rug was especially attractive to her. Her interest quickly turned to horror, however, when she discovered that on one end of the carpet there was a rectangular arrangement of "four well-worn indentations." It looked "exactly as though some heavy piece of furniture," perhaps a large four-poster rosewood bed, "had rested there for a matter of months."

Most of the people who attended that housewarming party have presumably gone to their own final reward without ever having publicly identified themselves as participants in this bizarre incident of retrocognition.

And what of the haunted house itself? The building was demolished, and a large apartment building now stands in its place. It would be interesting to know if any of the tenants have ever seen anything unexplainable in any of the suites.

In Vogue

In 1991, the Vogue Theatre on Granville Street in Vancouver, British Columbia, opened its doors once again. The once-grand Art Deco theatre had been abandoned for years before a group of talented and devoted people spent hundreds of hours restoring the place. Some of the necessary tasks were enormous while others were merely organizational, such as tidying various areas of the huge old building.

One afternoon during renovations, a woman took a moment to tidy a stack of old movie posters that had been found in a storeroom. The next morning, she found the posters had been taken off the shelf and spread around the floor, yet no one had been in the building overnight.

Perhaps that trick was a way of warning the living that the theatre was haunted—not long after that, the heavy fire doors would open and close seemingly of their own volition.

One summer's day, a technician was working on a platform high above the stage. The area was brutally hot, so the man was concentrating on his work in order to get down from his perch as quickly as possible. Suddenly the temperature of the air around him dropped dramatically. That is when he felt someone, or something, brush past him. And he wasn't the only one to feel an invisible presence brush by. The theatre's technical director had a similar encounter.

The operations manager occasionally had the uncomfortable sensation that someone was in the room with him when he knew he was alone. Once he turned to see who had come into the room, but all he saw was a misty shape in the doorway. On another occasion, he heard drums being played. He looked across the stage where the drums were set up, but there was no one near them. That afternoon as the employees were locking up for the night, the sound of drums echoed through the place once again. They all went back into the auditorium and looked up on the stage. There was no one near the drum set.

During a dance number in a 1995 production, a solid, lifelike figure suddenly appeared stage left. The image startled the performer so much that he had to cut his dance number short. After the show, he asked if anyone had been on stage with him. No one had, nor had anyone else seen the presence.

That evening at closing time, the technician who'd previously felt the ghost looked up at the projection booth and was surprised to see someone standing there. He was even more surprised to watch as the entity dissolved into nothingness before his eyes. When the performer and the technician compared details about the apparitions they'd seen, it was clear that they had both seen the same image.

No one knows who the ghost may have been when he was alive, but it's clear he's spending his afterlife in the Vogue Theatre.

Tranquille

The Tranquille Sanatorium: the name would be a demented irony if it were not for the fact that the institution took its name from the nearby Tranquille River. The old sanatorium was built in 1907 as a tuberculosis treatment centre, and the area just west of Kamloops in the province's interior became a company town of sorts.

Tuberculosis was often a fatal disease; many of the patients died over the years. Their bodies were discreetly transferred from the wards to the morgue through an intricate series of tunnels below the buildings' floors. The buildings are gone now, but it is said that chilling screams still echo through those abandoned tunnels.

Spirits on Tap

Haunted bars and nightclubs are probably a lot more common than the patrons of these establishments might like to acknowledge. A bar that once stood on East Pender Street in downtown Vancouver, British Columbia, is an excellent example.

This particular bar had been haunted since the establishment's owner died on the premises. It was always generally accepted that his spirit never left the building. The ghost was heard speaking on many occasions, and even when he was not heard, the staff could always tell when he was present because kitchen utensils and serving dishes would shake and bang against each other, making not only a supernatural sight but also an unearthly noise.

The entity liked to play with electrical appliances, and the industrial floor polisher was one of his favourite toys. When all else was quiet, the ghost would cause the polisher to turn on. As soon as the employees reacted with fright, he turned the machine off. But the workers weren't easily settled because they knew that the ghost's stunt would be followed by gales of ghostly laughter.

Only a very small piece of the ghost was ever actually seen, but that sighting was very officially documented—by the City of Vancouver police department. The incident took place as the bar manager was tallying up the night's receipts. As he worked, a movement caught his eye. The man looked up to see a disembodied hand floating through the air. Although previously a skeptic, the man readily admitted to "being a little nervous." He wasted no time in getting himself to the nearest police station. An officer accompanied him back into the building, but despite a thorough search, neither the hand nor any other part of the ghost was ever seen again.

CANADA'S NORTH

Klondike Kate

The gold rush—what heady days those must have been when gold was king.

Thousands of men gave up the comfort of their homes and families to join the hordes of prospectors snaking their way north in hopes of finding the mother lode—or at least a few shiny nuggets. Some did strike it rich, but far more failed completely. Others made their fortune only to lose it again, sometimes two or even three times over. The only people who consistently won at the gold rush game were those who stayed behind in boomtowns and effectively mined the miners. Storekeepers in those muddy makeshift communities stocked the necessary mining equipment; other entrepreneurs ran taverns where the lucky few could celebrate, and the not so fortunate could drown their sorrows.

Women were nearly as rare as gold in those towns, but some of the women who were there were wildly successful. Kathleen Eloisa Rockwell was one of those. Kathleen had been a chorus girl in New York City before the excitement of the gold rush lured her north. When she arrived in Dawson City, Yukon, however, she discovered there were no proper dancehalls or theatres. Fortunately, she'd brought enough money with her to tide her over while she reconsidered her options.

Soon Kate, as she had come to be called, met the handsome and ambitious young Alexander Pantages. He wasted no time in charming Kate into investing her money in a vaudeville theatre he intended to open. He envisioned offering live entertainment—dancers, singers, storytellers, actors, comedians, trained animals . . . pretty much any act that was willing to get up on stage and was at least mildly amusing. He was sure his idea would be a hit, and they opened the Orpheum Theatre. All went well for a time.

With the combination of Kate's capital and Alexander's eye for detail, the Orpheum Theatre prospered, aided by the impresario's habit of sweeping the theatre floor every night. It wasn't that he was overly concerned with cleanliness, he liked to pocket any gold nuggets the audience might have dropped.

Soon success went to Alexander's head, and he decided that he could do even better elsewhere. He left both the north and his partner, Kate, who had bankrolled his success. Soon the man owned a chain of theatres across Canada and into the United States. Unfortunately, he didn't foresee that a novelty known as the "movies" would soon replace live shows, and by the 1920s, his box-office receipts had begun to wane. By the time Alexander died in 1936, he was poor and unknown.

But what became of the woman he jilted? Klondike Kate never recovered from the heartbreak of having been cast aside by the man she had loved and supported. Despite her never-ending sorrow, Kate lived the rest of her long life in relative comfort.

By then the theatre in Dawson City that had brought both wealth and sorrow to its founders was in disrepair. The place was finally torn down in the 1960s. It was replaced with an exact replica, which aimed to make money by hosting tourists curious to learn more about the days of the gold rush.

Once the new building was complete, painters and carpenters began their work inside. These tradespeople often reported seeing what they described as "a very pretty lady" dressed in flamboyant outfits floating across the theatre's stage. Sometimes the entity would stare at the workers for a few moments before "disappearing into thin air." It seemed that Klondike Kate's spirit had returned to haunt the theatre she'd originally financed.

After all the finishing work on the new facility was completed, Parks Canada began running tours. At least one guide was well aware of Kate's lingering presence. As the guide was getting ready to leave one summer evening, she walked through the theatre to make sure that no one had stayed behind. She turned the house lights on to illuminate the auditorium and then walked across the stage, scanning to see if anyone had been left behind. The place seemed empty, until she looked to the left side of the second balcony. There stood Klondike Kate dressed in all her old-fashioned finery.

The sighting didn't frighten the staff member because she'd heard tales about the theatre being haunted. She even recognized the image from archival photographs she'd seen of Klondike Kate. If the ghost's flamboyant gown and distinctive red hair weren't enough proof of the haunting, the fact that the entity was ever so slightly transparent certainly would have been.

While walking away, Kate's presence stopped to look back. She smiled at the guide; then, in the blink of an eye, she vanished. Perhaps feeling accepted by the earthly woman who was maintaining "her" theatre, Kate began to appear more frequently. Initially the woman felt warmed when she saw the spirit, but after a few sightings she began to sense the ghost's great sorrow. This sensation, the woman reported, was so deep that she could not help being affected by it.

Although not everyone is as attuned to the spirit's presence as that guide was, Klondike Kate is widely accepted as an important part of the Orpheum Theatre in Dawson City, Yukon.

LaSalle's Haunted Cabin

In the late 1800s, the gold rush sent tens of thousands of men scurrying north. Some of them met an early death, while others came away with nothing but disappointment. Only a few actually found gold, which isn't surprising considering that very few of those prospectors knew anything about where they were going or what to do if they actually did make it to the goldfields.

Fred Nelson and his partner, who is only remembered by his last name, Swanson, managed to get to the Yukon, but by the time they did, the north's harsh winter had settled in. Either Nelson and Swanson didn't know any better or they were more stubborn than sensible, but despite the killing cold, they pushed on to a small settlement near the confluence of the Yukon and Forty Mile rivers. From there they ventured out searching for gold.

Near twilight, a snowstorm blew up. The already frigid temperature plummeted to life-threatening lows. Icy crystals whipped around them in blinding sheets. Which direction led back to their camp? It was impossible to tell, and in a blizzard as severe as this one, it would have been foolhardy to try to find the way. But spending that frigid night without shelter would have meant certain death.

Panic building, the men looked around, terrified that this would be their last day on earth. Then, just off in the distance, Nelson glimpsed something through the blowing snow. Was his mind playing tricks on him, or was there a small building ahead? Perhaps their lives would be spared. Fighting against the wind and blowing snow, the two men struggled toward this one glimmer of hope, praying that it wasn't merely a mirage.

Soon the shadowy outline of a cabin became clearer. Surely if the owner was at home, he would let them spend the night. The pair knocked on the door, but there was no answer. Then they pounded on the door with their mittened hands, calling as loudly as they could. Still there was no response. Swanson reached for the doorknob, hoping the cabin was unlocked, but Nelson grabbed his friend's hand and pulled it away from the door.

"That might be LaSalle's cabin," he warned.

At that time in the Yukon, the name LaSalle was enough to send shivers down anyone's spine. LaSalle was said to have been a miserable recluse with a vicious temper. No one in the area had ever had a pleasant interaction with the man, but even so, when he hadn't been seen for a number of weeks, a small group of men went into the bush to check on him. What they found was LaSalle's butchered body. They buried his bloodied remains near his cabin and then left the area as quickly as they could. They later told friends that the hermit's makeshift home had a decidedly uneasy feel to it.

No one ever volunteered to take on the task of tearing the old place down in case LaSalle's spirit still resided there. They reasoned that LaSalle's disposition had been nasty in life and likely would not have been improved by being viciously slashed to death by a killer that no one had bothered to hunt down.

As a result, when Nelson and Swanson found the place, the cabin had stood abandoned for more than a dozen years. During those years, anyone who had seen the cabin had given it a wide berth. Some even said they heard ghastly moans echoing from within.

But Swanson and Nelson didn't have a choice. They knew the cabin's unnatural reputation, but spending the night outside would bring certain death.

The two men opened the cabin door and called in. There was no answer, so they stepped inside. It wasn't much warmer, but they were grateful to be protected from the blowing snow.

The pair set down their gear and looked around. The cabin had two rooms, each with a window. After starting a small fire in the hearth, they closed the door to the second room to contain what little heat the flames might give. Both of the men felt uneasy, but eventually they fell asleep.

Several hours later, Nelson was awakened by what he thought was the sound of the wind howling around the log-frame house. He listened carefully and realized that it couldn't be the wind because it was coming from the second room in the cabin. A moment later Swanson was awake too. There was no question about it, the dreadful wailing noise was coming from inside the cabin, and the only way to describe the sound was moaning.

Marshalling their courage, they tried to open the door to the second room. It wouldn't budge. Hours before it had swung open easily. They tried and tried again. As they pushed and pulled against the door, the sounds changed from wails and moans to a man's barely audible voice crying out for help.

Nelson ran outside and around to the back of the cabin and peered into the window as best he could. The small room was filled with an eerie glow. He moved closer to the window and shielded his eyes with his hands. At the centre of the glow was a mist, a slightly transparent mist that looked remarkably like the shape of a man, a man with jagged, bloody slashes all over this body. Nelson bolted back around the cabin and ran inside.

The cries were an ear-splitting cacophony by now. There was no question in their minds; this was LaSalle's ghost. Showing great presence of mind, Swanson called out to the entity, asking if it was LaSalle's spirit. The noises stopped, and all was quiet for a heartbeat. Then the cabin walls vibrated with a thump as though from an enormous fist. Taking this as an answer from the great beyond, Swanson asked more questions; each was answered with a knock on the wall.

But when Swanson asked the presence who had murdered him, the door between the cabin's two rooms burst open and the doorway was filled with the apparition of a man covered in blood.

Swanson and Nelson grabbed what they could of their gear and ran from the cabin as fast as their shaky legs would carry them through the deep snow.

Nelson eventually described their terrifying encounter to a reporter with the *Klondike Nugget*, who didn't bother to go out to LaSalle's cabin to confirm the facts. He merely accepted Nelson's statement as true, later commenting, "No one could pretend to be that scared."

It's fun to wonder, from the safety of our warm, comfortable homes, whether or not LaSalle's cabin is still standing, and if it is, whether or not it is still haunted by a nasty ghost seeking revenge.

Rest in Peace

Augustus Richard Peers died on March 15, 1853, at Fort McPherson in what is now the Northwest Territories. His fellow Hudson's Bay Company traders knew that Peers did not want to be buried at Fort McPherson. Despite this, Roderick MacFarlane, his immediate superior, ordered that the man be laid to rest where he died.

It wasn't until December of 1859 that MacFarlane decided to honour his dead colleague's request. Digging down into the frozen soil was back-breaking work, but MacFarlane was determined to move the body to Fort Simpson, some 300 kilometres away, using the only transportation available: dogsled.

But the coffin the men had hastily built for the man in 1853 would not be nearly sturdy enough to make the journey. They would have to make a stronger one and transfer the body.

Once all of this was accomplished, the men at the fort began the gruesome task of prying open the original coffin. What lay inside was a dreadful shock. The body hadn't decayed at all. MacFarlane described the body as being "in much the same condition as shortly after the day of his death."

The sight unnerved everyone at the fort, but the men who were going to accompany the dogsled carrying the body to its final destination were especially upset. Nevertheless they set out on their difficult mission, traversing, as MacFarlane later described, "over the rugged masses of tossed-up ice along the mighty Mackenzie River." The coffin and the team's provisions were packed on the sled while the men, wearing snowshoes, walked.

By the time the party reached Fort Good Hope, more than 600 kilometres from their starting place, the men and the dogs were exhausted. MacFarlane was concerned that if they didn't make some changes, none of them would make it to their destination alive. Somehow they needed to lighten their load, but there was nothing they could safely dispense with—except the heavy coffin containing the body. And so, for the second time since his death, Peers was removed from his coffin. This time, however, his remains were simply wrapped in a sheet.

When the men reached the next fort they rested again, knowing that the last leg of their journey would be the longest. MacFarlane described their routine during the trip saying that they got underway each morning by three or four o'clock. At noon they stopped for food and an hour's break, then they stopped at nightfall.

One night, the dogs would not settle while the group set up camp. The animals were barking and clearly agitated. The men knew these dogs well, and this behaviour was out of the ordinary. One of the men, perhaps more sensitive than the others, remarked that animals often sense supernatural presences more easily than people do. It was then that they heard a human voice calling out a single word, "march," over and over again.

The men searched the area, hoping to find the person who had spoken, but there was no one there. The dogs were becoming even more restless. Then, as suddenly as the animals' ruckus had started, it stopped. The dogs lay down and fell asleep for the night.

The next three days all went well for both animals and men until they heard a voice speak that single word again: "march." They searched as they had before, but there simply wasn't anyone else there.

The group set out on the final leg of their journey early the next morning, arriving at Fort Simpson in the afternoon. They lost no time in building a third coffin for the frozen body. Two days later they buried it in the Hudson's Bay Company graveyard.

As MacFarlane and the rest of the tired men relaxed in the fort that evening, they told the other traders about their journey. After a moment's hesitation, they also mentioned the disembodied voice that they had heard. One of the men listening had known Peers very well. He imitated the man's style of speech when he was ordering a team of dogs forward. "March," he called, exactly the way the travellers had heard it during their arduous trek. A hush fell over the men. Could they have heard a ghost's voice? The very thought of such a thing brought the conversation to a halt. Soon the men dispersed and went to bed for the night.

MacFarlane was in a deep sleep when he woke to find the ghost of Augustus Peers standing next to him. The man sleeping in the bunk opposite sat up. He could see the apparition too. Both men turned away from the image and pulled the covers up over their head. By morning the ghost was gone.

In 1913, more than fifty years after the experience, MacFarlane wrote about seeing the spirit of his long-deceased colleague, saying that he regretted having passed up his only opportunity to communicate with the dead.

As for Peers, we can only hope that he rested as peacefully at Fort Simpson as he had at Fort McPherson because it is clear that the arduous journey between the two forts unsettled his soul.

Twelve Stranded Men

Taloyoak, or Spence Bay as it was called until 1992, sits on a hillside at the southern end of the Boothia Peninsula in Nunavut, Canada's newest territory. This tiny village is 3,000 kilometres north of the Arctic Circle and overlooks the frigid waters of the St. Roch Basin.

In November 1971, twelve representatives from the territorial and federal governments were sent to Spence Bay on an information-gathering mission. Hours before the contingent was to fly out of this remote settlement, a severe arctic storm blew through the area, completely cutting the community off from the rest of the world and stranding the civil servants in what was to them a very strange land.

While the storm raged across the barren stretch of snow and ice, the residents of the hamlet extended gracious hospitality and shared their spartan accommodations with their marooned guests. If any of the visitors were not already distressed by the unfamiliar and potentially life-threatening situation they found themselves in, then being entertained by local ghost stories no doubt pushed them strongly in that direction.

According to a newspaper report in the *Edmonton Journal* on November 25, 1971, Ernest Lyall, who had lived in the North for most of his life, began by "casually" mentioning to the stranded men that the Hudson's Bay Company building they were sheltered in was haunted—haunted by the ghost of a murdered woman. The crime had taken place in winter some years before, just outside the community. A timely burial was impossible as the ground was frozen. Lyall remembered that he and some others brought the corpse into the building instead, where it lay until spring.

Interestingly, evidence of the haunting began immediately after the funeral. "We were just starting to sit down for dinner one evening when the outer door opened, and we heard footsteps coming into the room." Next, they heard a person clearing their throat.

The stranded city folk were all ears as the man continued, speaking loudly enough to be heard over the gales blowing around and through the building. "We went to see who it was, but there was nobody there." Even so, the disembodied footsteps followed by the distinctive sound of the throat clearing continued for many nights.

Lyall then recounted the time that he'd hidden in the dining room, hoping to catch the prankster he presumed was walking around and clearing his throat. The man hid for half an hour, listening to the sounds and seeing no one; he finally gave up and went back to the table to finish his meal. He had no sooner sat down than he heard the door opening again. The phantom sounds went on "for the rest of the winter," the man acknowledged. "The people of this community say it is the spirit of the murdered woman," he added.

The small audience shivered as he concluded the tale by assuring everyone gathered that the ghost has never left the building.

Other members of the visiting group gathered at the local teacherage, where a woman from the community spoke to the visitors about a vicious fight that had taken place in the early 1900s between supernatural beings and a respected shaman. In order to set the scene, the woman first explained that, in those days, each family built and lived in an "ice house." A clear block of ice formed a portion of the roof of each structure; it was selected specifically to allow light from the outside into the living area. Each individual residence was linked to the dwelling on either side by way of a tunnel, thereby forming a chain of houses.

In the year the story took place, the community's shaman was experiencing terrible interference from the spirits of his predecessors. These deceased leaders and spiritual healers either did not approve of the way shaman was carrying out his responsibilities, or perhaps, even in death, they were not willing to relinquish the important positions they had held.

One winter's day, as all the residents watched in fear, the shaman did physical battle with the ghosts of his forefathers. The fight went on for hours. Although the ghostly shamans were not visible to anyone but the living shaman, the woman relating the tale recalled that as the spirits moved from house to linked house, their shadows blocked out the light streaming in through the clear piece of ice in each roof.

The visitors listening to this story may, at first, have taken it to be a fanciful piece of folklore, until the woman telling the tale acknowledged that she had been a witness to the struggle. The shaman had come away from the altercation suffering from deep knife wounds on his arms and scalp. Even the most skeptical southerners had a difficult time discounting such graphic evidence of the otherworldly altercation.

When the storm eventually cleared, the plane scheduled to pick up the twelve men finally arrived at the airstrip. They all headed back south with some unique and eerie memories of their time in Canada's Far North.

Frozen in Time

A phantom ship is the image of a vessel still sailing after the physical ship has gone to its watery afterlife. A floating apparition like this is routinely referred to as a *"Flying Dutchman,"* a reference to the first recorded phantom ship. Canada's coastlines are home to many of these frightening manifestations, but there are also tales from inland areas.

Whitehorse is situated on the Yukon River south of Lake Laberge, and it is home to a phantom river steamer. Some folklore buffs speculate that the eerie image might be that of the original *Klondike*, a riverboat that ran aground in 1936 on the Yukon River between Lake Laberge and the Teslin River.

The phantom riverboat often sails along the lake, heading toward the Yukon River. Many credible witnesses have been fascinated to see boat's sudden appearance—followed by her equally sudden disappearance.

In the summer of 1981, three couples stood together on the shore of Lake Laberge and watched the apparition. All six people confirmed that the vessel was a large, sand-coloured sternwheeler. Then they watched in amazement as the spectre became somewhat misty until finally, starting with the bow, the vessel vanished as mysteriously as it had appeared.

Over the years there have been many similar sightings. Those who've seen the phantom are consistently frustrated that they can see a name painted on the side of the ship's pilot house, but not quite well enough to read it. Some people have even reported seeing passengers milling about on the steamer's deck. All the witnesses know that the craft is not of this world because instead of creating a wave in its wake, the enigmatic vessel trails a phosphorescent glow. And as the ship approaches sandbars, it seems to levitate just enough to easily glide over them.

The riverboat was apparently a remarkable sight when it was in service, but it would certainly be an even *more* remarkable sight today.

Wendigo

Cautionary tales are stories that warn us away from unacceptable or hazardous activities. Given that the climate in Canada's Far North can be life-threatening, it's no surprise that there are so many supernatural tales from the territories reflecting those inherent dangers.

One of the most chilling tales involves a threatening creature known as the Wendigo. When communities are suffering, the Wendigo can overcome even the bravest, strongest member. Once possession takes hold, the victim's eyes become blank, as though there is no life left in them. Once Wendigo has established itself in a host body, the victim becomes a cannibal.

Clearly this tale is a warning against eating human flesh, no matter how dire times might be.

Shadow People

A traditional tale told in Nunavut concerns spirits known as the shadow people, or *Taqriaqsuit*. These souls are terrifying, even though they are rarely seen. They follow a person making his or her way across the snow-covered land and manifest as miniature blizzards trailing behind a traveller, instantly filling in the person's footsteps.

Some people claim to have glimpsed the mysterious entities, but such sightings are rare. Others have been terrified when they heard the creatures' voices and laughter. These shadow people travel in groups, and in at least one instance, have used a sled dog team. A man who witnessed that eerie manifestation told his family that he ran toward the image and jumped on the sled, but he found himself lying on the snow with nothing, certainly no sled and team, anywhere around him.

Perhaps this tale warns people not to go too far from home when conditions are perilous.

Bushman

In 2016, the tiny community of Trout Lake in the Northwest Territories officially changed its name to Sambaa K'e, which means "place of trout" in the Dehcho language. The population of Sambaa K'e is about a hundred people, and most of the year those souls are cut off from the rest of the world, except by air. Despite the difficult access, Sambaa K'e is a popular destination for travellers who enjoy the pristine beauty of the rugged outdoors and are anxious to fish in the rich waters of the northern wilderness.

During the late 1960s and into the early 1970s, Trout Lake, as it was known then, was haunted by a very strange entity known as Nakhah, or bushman. The manifestation was larger than any of the men in the community and often had a dog walking with him. The creature was clearly aware of the living and actually tried to trick people into coming close to him by playing dead.

One day a brother and sister were carrying home bundles of chopped wood when they saw Nakhah lying on the ground. Thinking it was a man in need of help, the children approached the still form. Just as they did, the phantom jumped up and ran toward them. The children dropped the wood they'd been carrying and ran away as fast as they could with the apparition and his dog following at their heels.

After that, more people reported seeing the phantom. Occasionally he would even approach their homes and stare in the windows. Some villagers thought he was a living man, but others argued that no human being could live outside in such extreme cold.

Trout Lake's leaders tried to calm the people's fears. It might have been helpful except that their chief also saw the Nakhah. He followed the strange image and called out to it offering assistance in the form of food or clothing, but there was no reply. The chief admitted that he was frightened by the encounter and no longer denied the existence of the eerie presence. Over the next five years, the Nakhah haunted these hardy northerners before vanishing as mysteriously as he had arrived. Happily, he has never been seen since.

An even more peculiar incident was described in a 1916 edition of the *Nome Nugget* newspaper.

One winter, mining engineer Don Mack was working at Tagish Lake, a narrow body of water that straddles the border between the Yukon and British Columbia. When he and his colleagues camped on Bove Island for the night, Mack dreamed that a woman named Ethel Williams of Syracuse, New York, advised him not to follow through on his plans to travel in a particular direction the next day. The snow-covered ice was thin there, the woman explained to the sleeping man.

He told his colleagues about his odd dream the next morning and recommended that they head out in a different direction. The other men laughed and made fun of Mack, but he wasn't dissuaded. He detoured the area he'd been warned about. The other men went ahead as planned.

Several days after Mack reached his destination the others still hadn't arrived, so he organized a search party. All they found were empty canoes and a few supplies floating on the frigid lake close to the area he had been warned about in his dream.

Mack's memories of his co-workers and the strange dream he had experienced tormented him, and he had to find out if there was such a person as Ethel Williams living in Syracuse, New York. Much to his surprise, there was. He wrote Mrs. Williams a letter thanking her for saving his life. The woman was so astonished by Mack's letter that she submitted the story to her local newspaper, and the *Nome Nugget* picked it up from there. She declared that she had never met anyone by the name of Don Mack, and furthermore, she had never heard of Tagish Lake!

It's anyone's guess what might have caused Mack's uncanny dream, but until the day he died, of natural causes, he was grateful that he had heeded the strange warning.

Benign Bessie

In 1908, when Bessie and Edwin Gideon took over the Caribou Hotel in Carcross, Yukon, the building was only ten years old. Yet, it already had an interesting history. It was floated from the community of Bennett, down the lake of the same name, to its new location at Carcross. The move was hardly worth the effort, though, because the wooden structure caught fire and burned to the ground the following year. The Gideons were apparently not quitters because they rebuilt the hotel and reopened it.

The unusual history continued in 1918, when Captain James Alexander and his pet parrot, Polly, moved into the hotel. A few months later the captain drowned in the sinking of the *Sophia*. Everyone at the hotel had grown very fond of the quirky bird, which not only requested a cracker but a drop of liquor too. It's been said that the bird even knew operatic arias. When the clever and beloved bird died, it was buried in the local cemetery with its grave respectfully marked. The bird's life and death must have been entirely satisfying because he has rested in peace ever since.

The same cannot be said of Bessie Gideon, whose life was virtually devoted to the Caribou. Her spirit has lingered in the hotel since her death in 1933. Bessie is a benign but active spirit. Guests often see her standing at the end of their bed before she vanishes as mysteriously as she arrived. She's heard closing doors in empty parts of the hotel and when the floorboards squeak in an empty hallway, everyone knows that Bessie is just making her rounds in the afterlife—as she did in her real life.

Rude Wraith

At the Westminster Hotel in Dawson City, Yukon, a ghost knocks on doors at the most inconvenient times and then impatiently rattles the doorknob. It's presumed that this nuisance of a ghost is the same phantom that people often see just out of the corner of their eye. He is easy to recognize, wearing a jaunty fedora. The ghost has been blamed for picking up a cell phone that someone had left on the piano and throwing it across the room. As the hotel is known for its live music, perhaps the ghost is the spirit of a former musician.

Acknowledgements

Thanks always to Rodger and Pat Touchie. Thanks to Taryn Boyd, publisher at TouchWood Editions, for embracing and supporting this project. Thanks, too, to Tori Elliott, Renée Layberry, Colin Parks, and Claire Philipson.

And to those closest to me, my family and friends, thank you so much for being who you are. I need you in my life.

Bibliography

Aykroyd, Peter H. with Narth, Angela. (2009). *A History of Ghosts, The True Story of Seances, Mediums, Ghosts and Ghostbusters.* New York, NY: Rodale Inc.

Butts, Edward. (2010). *Ghost Stories of Newfoundland and Labrador,* Toronto, ON: Dundurn Press.

Christensen, Jo-Anne. (1995). *Ghost Stories of Saskatchewan.* Toronto, ON: Hounslow Press.

Cleary, Val. (1985). *Ghost Stories of Canada,* Toronto, ON: Hounslow Press.

Colby, C.B. (1959). *Strangely Enough.* New York, NY: Sterling Publishing.

Colombo, John Robert. (1985). *Ghost Stories of Canada.* Toronto, ON: Hounslow Press.

Forsberg, Lois. (1998). *Prairie Ghosts, True Manitoba Ghost Stories.* Brandon, MB: Elf Publications.

Fraser, Mary L. (n.d.). *Folklore of Nova Scotia.* Antigonish, NS: Formac Limited.

Kirby, William. (1877). *The Golden Dog.* Montreal, PQ: Lovell, Adams, Wesson and Company.

Leslie, Mark & Jelen, Jenny. (2013). *Spooky Sudbury, True Tales of the Eerie and Unexplained.* Toronto, ON: Dundurn.

Myers, Frederic. (1903, 1961). *Human Personality and Its Survival of Bodily Death.* New Hyde Park, NY: University Books, Incorporated.

Ogden, Tom. (2009). *Haunted Theaters, Playhouse Phantoms, Opera House Horrors and Backstage Banshees.* Guilford, CT: Globe Pequot Press.

Ronan, Margaret. (1974). *Strange Unsolved Mysteries.* New York, NY: Scholastic Publishing.

Sinn, Shannon. (2017). *The Haunting of Vancouver Island: Supernatural Encounters with the Other Side,* Victoria, BC, TouchWood Editions.

Skelton, Robin & Kozocari, Jean. (1989). *A Gathering of Ghosts.* Saskatoon, SK: Western Producer.

Smith, Barbara. (1998). *Ghost Stories of Manitoba.* Edmonton, AB: Lone Pine Publishing.

Smith, Barbara. (1998). *Ontario Ghost Stories.* Edmonton, AB: Lone Pine Publishing.

Smith, Barbara. (2002). *Haunted Theaters.* Edmonton, AB: Ghost House Books.

Sutherland, Dawn. (2015). *Murder and Mayhem, Canadian Ghost Stories.* Edmonton, AB: Quagmire Press.

Traill, Catherine Parr. (1836). *The Backwoods of Canada,* Charles Knight, London, England. Facsimile edition reprinted (1971) Coles Publishing Company, Toronto.

Trueman, Stuart. (1975). *Ghosts, Pirates and Treasure Trove, The Phantoms that Haunt New Brunswick.* Toronto, ON: McClelland and Stewart Limited.

Upton, Kyle. (1999). *Niagara's Ghosts 2, Niagara's Ghosts at Fort George* (2004) St. Catharines, ON: Privately published.

BARBARA SMITH is the author of over thirty-five books, including *Campfire Stories of Western Canada*, *The Famous Five*, *The Valiant Nellie McClung*, *Hoaxes and Hexes*, *The Mad Trapper*, and perennial bestsellers *Ghost Stories of Alberta*, *Ghost Stories and Mysterious Creatures of British Columbia*, and *Ghost Stories of the Rocky Mountains*. Barbara's lifelong dream was to become a writer, and it was her love of history and mystery that led her to specialize in supernatural folklore. Born and raised in Toronto, she left Ontario for Edmonton, Alberta, where she endured many cold prairie winters before finally settling in Sidney, BC.